Moon Eclipse, Days of Darkness

Jean Marie Rusin

authorHOUSE®

AuthorHouse™
1663 Liberty Drive
Bloomington, IN 47403
www.authorhouse.com
Phone: 1-800-839-8640

Published by AuthorHouse   1/26/2012

ISBN: 978-1-4685-4207-3 (sc)
ISBN: 978-1-4685-4206-6 (e)

Other Books by Jean Marie Rusin:

Long Silky Blonde Girl

Thin Ice Zombies in LA Nowhere to run or hide (Returns)
Thin Ice Zombies In LA Nowhere to run or hide.
Broken Bridge lies body of water
Detour
Willow lakes Hauntings!
Nights of terror
A polish Christmas story with a magical Christmas tree.

Contents

Kate and Joe first date 1

Freak accident 4

Break up 8

No Family ties 12

Surgery 14

Left Town 16

Rachel and Joe 18

Rachel goes to Manhattan NY 20

Joe and Rachel Wedding day! 22

Left Hawaii on the earlier flight 26

Leo move out stalk by Kate 29

Joe and Rachel the Halloween Party 32

Halloween October 31, ... 35

Day one lights out 38

Day two lights out 40

Day three lights out 42

Day five lights out 46

Day six lights out 48

Seventh day of lights out 50

Eighth day lights out 52

Epidemic 54

Searching for other survivors 57

Moon Eclipse 59

Mayhem and death and no end of Zombies 61

Infection spread coast to coast 67

Fighting for your life 69

Is this the end of the world? 71

Long ways from home 73

Mist 76

Night of dead   80
In the dark   82
Three hours, to get home   85
"Night of the Storm"   87
Meteor Shower   89
Coming out of the graves   94
Zombie girl   96
Jack and Jamie last journey   98
History of Zombies   102
Destroy the evidence about zombies   105
The remains   109
The zombies are breaking in!!!   111
Acid Rain   113
House of Zombies   115
Ah! Zombies, Ah ! Zombies Dogs coming this ways!   117
Escape from Zombies   119
Heading to Texas zone free of Zombies   121
Ambush   124
Shelter surrounded by Zombies   127
"Bright Lights"   129
The Long Journey unknown   131
End of the epidemic   133
Going Home   136
Old creepy house   138
Dark Shadows in the old creepy house   140
Destination   142
Alone in the woods, went back to the house   144
Daylight   148
Heading home with a dead body   150
Midnight   152
Terror in the street   154
Night of the comet   157
Lost Girl   159
Darkest Hours   161
Pitch Black   163
Strict Area (Do Not Enter)   165

Zombies Territory   168
Mores Flashing Lights   170
Apocalypse Zombies   172
Air Raid and sirens   174
Six month later   176
Unknown origin   179
One survive   182

"Moon Eclipse, days of darkness

By Jean Marie Rusin

*Edited by K. D

Kate and Joe first date

On the first date of Kate and Joe, they knew that they belong together, and Joe was in love at first sight with Kate, and Kate felt the same.

That night Kate and Joe spend the whole night talking about how they felt for each others and Joe didn't wanted to let her go but Kate had to go to work the next morning and Joe said I will walks you to the door and Kate said that is okay! I will be fine, but he still walks her to the door and gave her a kiss on the lips and didn't want to let her go!

After that Joe left Kate came inside the house and her parents were waiting up for her, and Kate was smiling and happy and they knew that Kate was in love with Joe, and Joe drove all the ways home thinking of Kate, and when he got home, he when inside his home and locked the door and he thought to himself that he needed to called Kate before he went to sleep, and he was happy that night, and Kate was speaking to her parents about Joe and said, I wants to be with this man the rest of my life, and her mom said, daughter don't rush into, be sure and I am sure mom about how I feel about this man, and then the phone rang and it was Joe and Kate spoke to him and they make plan to sees each others tomorrow night and Kate mom said are seeing him again? and Kate said yes I am think that I love him, but dear you only met him today and you are not in love and how do you know that I am not? But mom it is love at first sight and it never happened before, but honey don't rush into anything just take your time with Joe, once you thought that you were in love and he ran off with your friend Karen, I don't remember and why are you bringing this up, don't you wants me to be happy? Of course I do! But sometime it seems like you don't, Kate when into her room and when into the bedroom and locked the door and thought about Joe and that night Kate couldn't sleep.

Kate got up and walks around and then she decided to called Jim but then she just hung up the phone before it rang, and she lay down on the bed and dreamt about Joe that night, and meanwhile Joe was getting ready for bed and his ex girlfriend Kelly called and said I wants to sees you and Jim said well you know it is over and I don't wants too sees you again! We were great together and why are you doing this too me? Well I met someone special; and I will ask her to married me? You must be joking you don't want to be marry, you only wants to have sex and then you just don't bother with them again! probably in the past but not with Kate, I just feel something special with her, I don't wants to hears that Joe, once I was special to you and you don't want me to tell her about your past. So you are blackmailing me too sees you it not going too work and then Joe hung up the phone and then Kelly got furious and said I will fix you and you will pays for it and your new girlfriend will know what you wants from her and then you dump her, when you get her money, and then you have sex. Now Joe was a bit frighten what Kelly said, and he thought and said, Kelly were not do something stupid and break me up with Kate, and then he fell asleep and the next morning he called Kate and wanted to says "good morning" and then Kate answers and said I am on my ways to work and I will meet you at Jake at five pm tonight after work and Jim wanted to says I need to tell you something but Kate said I am running late just tell me later and Joe said " I Love you" and Kate said " I love you too! And then Kate said bye and I will see you later! They both hung up and Joe was worry about Kelly, ruining his relationship with Kate.

Later that day, Joe called Kelly and said meet me at our old place and Kelly said what was the turned around well we needed to talked, fine!

Meanwhile Kate at work was not really paying attention what she was doing and then her boss said what wrong with you well I think I find my new love, you don't says? Well hope that you are right? I am about him and he feels the same about me, are you sure? Yes I am, Bob, and Kate walks out of the office and went to her desk and was about to called Joe but her mom called and said her brother was in an accident in Vermont and Kate need to comes home immediately, and Kate said what happen to him it was a ski accident and you hit his head and he is in ICU. No! What happened, well he was drinking and skiing and somehow he hit the tree when he was going down that great! Now I need to cancel my date with Joe, yes you do and you and I and your dad are driving up too Vermont, do I have too go?

Yes, how many times do I have to tell you, we don't know the road to the hospital, ok I will asked my boss Bob to let me go because it is a family emergency, yes indeed. They alls drove to the hospital and Kate called to Jim and said "I have a family crisis and I will be back in five days and sorry that I cancel the date and I will call you when I get back.

Later that night Joe got the message and said good I am clear and I can fix Kelly and tell her to leave me alone, that night when he met up with Kelly, they started to talks and Kelly started to talks about how good they were and then something happened and Joe push her and she fell and hit her head and it was bleeding, and Joe ran up to her and said sorry, but I didn't wanted to hurt you, and then Kelly got up and started to hit him and said you are going to pays, why are you so crazy, we didn't works and you are still stalking me? I really love you, but we didn't work don't you understand, I do, but you hurt my heat and then she fell to the ground, and then Joe said what have I done and then he called the ambulance and they took her to the hospital and he was on her side all the ways and then when they arrives at the hospital and he told them what happened and then he sat next to her bed all night, and meanwhile Kate her family arrives in Vermont, to sees his brother in ICU.

Freak accident

Kate and her family when inside the ICU and her brother was on the breathing machine and so far he didn't wake up and meanwhile Kelly bedside and Joe and holding her hands and said I am sorry what I did and then she woke up and said I have a bad headache and then Joes said I needs to called Kate and Kelly said don't leave me I won't be long I promise you, okay! Joe, I will be right back, so Joe step out and called Kate but her cell when to voice mail immediately and Joe said, when you get back we should get together and I Love you, and hung up. Later that night Joe sat near Kelly and they talked about how things didn't work out, and Jim said I still love you and I don't hate you and I don't neither, but I will go along with you, but I will not cause anymore problem. But we can be friend, but Joe I want to be more than that but we tried but it didn't work so it is time for us too, move on, that is true, said Kelly and Joe

Kelly said was out of line and I wants to apology about trying to blackmail you and you don't feel the same and I do understand it is time too let go! I will not threaten you again, and will you forgive me? Yes but please don't do it again! I won't and then that night Joe left and when home and called Kate and she didn't answered the phone and meanwhile in Vermont, her brother was in critical condition and the doctor said his chancing are slim and Kate left the room and was crying that her brother might died, and her parents needed to make a decision what to do? But then Kate parents came out ands said that we will send him to a special hospital for care and when he woke up and we will be back with us again! Then Kate and her family stay near the hospital and Kate was too upset to talks with Joe and so she shut down her cell and kept with her parents about her brother and they went to church to pray for him too get well,, and Kate said to her mom I will called my boss Bob and tells him that I will have a leave of absent for a month and her mom and dad said, no you should go back to Manhattan and get back to your job, no I don't want too leaves you and dad and my brother, we will be fine, no I am not going, don't be stubborn, I am not, yes you are and Ben were not wants you too lose your job, fine. So I will be latter leaving on the late train to Manhattan that leaving at 10 pm and Joe will meet me at the grand central station and then he will stayed with me and is that alls right mom and dad, we really don't like it but it he gets you home safe that alls it counts, yes you are right dear, and once again Kate when into her brother room and said I would stay but I need to get back to my job and I will thinking of you, Ben, and then her parents drove her to the train station and then she got on the train and the train move and she was leaving Vermont and her Parents got back into the car and drove back to the hospital and later that night Kate got nearer to the train station and Joe was waiting for her when she step out and then went she saw him and he saw her, he grab her and gave her a kiss and said "comes home with me" tonight! I cannot I need to go back to my home and you can join me and he said, I shall do that, and they took a cab from the train station to fifth Ave and said, are you sure that your parents did allow this, ? yes I am., come on in., and Joe did and they sat on the couch and then he kiss her an d she kiss him back and then he carry her into the bedroom and they make love that night. Then the phone rang and it was Kate mom and dad and her dad said are you alone and Kate said "dad I am not a child anymore and why are you treating me that's? Then Kate asked her dad about Ben and he said it doesn't looks good and Kate said should I comes back and he answers and said no stay in Manhattan, fine dad and how is mom doing not that great and she is worry about your brother, I know dad, but I will be fine and so called me if something happened, sure I will be you cannot be with your boyfriend, in our home alone and do you understand, Kate? Sure dad I do!

After Kate was finished with her dad on the phone said to Jim, you need to go and then he said, well I guess you're still a child, what do you means? Well your dad said you cannot have anyone here when they are not around so I will leaves, don't be mad, well you are acting like a child, no I am not said Kate,, and now Kate got mad and said go and I don't want too sees you again!!! Fine and he got dress and left her room and then he left the house and Kate, started to cried and thought to her what have I done.

About one hour later, Jim called and said I am so, so, sorry that I got angry at you, I didn't means what I said too you and then Kate listen to him and he said will you sees me tomorrow at lunch near Central park and she said I will tried to be there, and he said I wants to sees you and I wants to hold you in my arms, and then Kate said well I forgive you and I will be more independent, but I like you has you are and don't change, please don't you are the best thing ever happen in my life and you are precious too me, come on now you going over board and stops that I will and I wants to sees you tomorrow, you will! I love you so do I! then he hung up the phone and smile and said I have her and I will not ruins my chances and I need to tell her about my past, and I ,know that she will not have this against me, and then he when into the den and his younger brother Leo said did you tell her that you were arrest for assault your girlfriend in Connecticut, no I have not and she will never know, but Kelly will tell her and but she promise that she won't and you took her word, yes I did, fine I think she will tell her and you will lose Kate for good,, so why are you so negative, well we were raise by abuse parents and now we have there personality and now we are stuck and behaving like t hey are and we were taken from them and we were place into foster care and we also got abuse and it is not ours faults and I think that if we got help we would never end up in prisoner, that is true.

But that how the deck was deal and we just got into trouble and we were young! But I hope that Kate does not go against you and doesn't want you in her life. I don't wants to hears that Leo but I know I need to be honest with her and she will not get rid of her life and I know that she love me and that is alls we need., well I hope that your right!

But will she believe you once you would a con man and were in prisoner for five years and then I know that you tried to change but it was not easy for you, Joe but you time serve your time and now you have a good job and you met a wonderful girl and she is in love with you so you cannot go wrong, I know but the past will catch up too me and I need to tells her before her dad investigates my past and then she will not sees me anymore, that is true.

But Leo you know that I have change, and I am not the same man that I was before so, hope that her family will accept me when someday I asked Kate to be my wife, I don't know Joe but I hope that you have a chance and the parents think that you are after there money and but that is not true and I love Kate,, so now your going have to prove it to them and not hide anything, from Kate and try to keep Kelly away and but Leo she promise that she were not tell and you trust her and Joe said, I do. You do believe her and you must be kidding me, she even stalk you and you still have her in your life, well she didn't have a good life with her family neither so, I need to be her friend, and don't let Kate find out that you are still seeing your ex girlfriend and she will leave you, and you promise not too tell her, I won't and I will just be quiet and listens to whatever you says, well I will be seeing Kate tonight and her brother is still in ICU and has a head injury and he might recover and I am sure what to says to her but ;last night were together but she refuse to comes to my place but I stay with her at her parents house and then I left and I have not heard from her yet! But I know that she will be going to Vermont and I might be going with her too.

Break up

J oe called Kate but she couldn't talked right now and Joe was not sure what was going on, but Joe was getting worry and he knew that Kate was not herself and didn't wants to speak with Jim and he tried but she refuse and hung up the phone, and before she did she said don't calls me again, if you do you will be arrested, and Joe said for what? You being a stalker, please talked too me, I will explains everything too you and I don't wants to hears from you again! then Kate hung up the phone and Joe sat down and took a bottle of vodka and took a glass and pour in and drank and about two hours later, Leo came in and said what wrong, well somehow Kate find out about me being in prisoner and she doesn't wants too sees me, I told you too be honest with her and now you have lost her, I will get her back, well I don't want you too get arrested and you will and they are powerful peoples, and you don't have chance, do you understand? Yes I do but I love Kate and I want her, do you know how you are sounding, crazy, yes but love make you that ways, well so far I didn't have anyone like Kate. Later that night Jim said I am driving to her house,, well I cannot let you go, you are asking for trouble, I don't care I wants to be with her,, well you end up in prisoner for five years if you go there and stalk her, and maybe even gets shot.

My life with Kate, I have nothing well you still have Kelly, but Kelly and I am only friend and that alls, do you hears what I am saying too you? Yes loud and clears, well shut up and I don't wants anything from your big mouth too comes out. Leo said fine, I am going and I will see you the morning and I will hang out with Star. Go Leo and Joe kept drinking and then fell asleep and then the phone rang and then it was Kelly.

Jim said I don't wants to talk s with you now so leave me alone and then Kelly said I am coming over you need a friend and I will there in half hour fine and then she hung up the phone and then Joe fell asleep and then the doorbell rang and it was Kelly. Joe woke up and answered the door and opens the door, it was Kelly and what are you doing here? I told you that I was coming over, don't remember what I told you, okay I remember but you are drunk, yes I am... then Kelly took him into the shower, I don't need one, yes you do! But Joe didn't wanted too listens to Kelly and walks out and locks the door behind him. But then Kelly, said comes out and we will talks, fine, what are you going to says that it were not works between us because we are from different world, no we love each others and now, she won't even listens what I have too says, well you should have told her about your past but you kept it a secret and you got burned.

I know that your right but I do know that she still loved me but now she is not taking my called and she told me not to call her again and it is over.

But I need her to sees me who I am not who I have been, but I need to talks with her alone and make her understand, well she known who you are and what you have done in the past and she is afraid of it and her parents don't like you and they make her sees what you are, I am human and I did make mistake and I pays for it and now I am not that person, not anymore, I have change and I would not hurt anyone in my life, but you have a criminal record of assault with a deadly weapon, yes I know , I was young and I hung out with the wrong crowds, well Kate is not the type were hang out with a man from the other side of town, and you didn't have a silver spoon when you were born but she did, and it were never works, and stops saying that's but Joe it is true, I don't wants to hears it and you need to talked with her, I am not going to stalks her because of you, you owe me, I do and you hurt me in the past, with your friends, so you have revenge in your eyes, no I just don't wants to be part of your dilemma. I do understand, but I think that I will leaves you alone, but stay with me, no I don't wants to be used by you, I just wants to talks with you, that alls!

So Kelly stay and listened to what Joe was saying and then Kelly gave him a hug and then he kissed her, and then Kelly push him away and got up and said I am going so, I am not staying, and Joe got up and kissed her lips and then she kissed him back and then he pick her up and took her into the bedroom and lay her on the bed and remove her blouse and she unzipped his pants, and then they make love, and then the phone rang, and it was Leo and he said that he is at the police station got busted for a drug deal and Jim said why are you getting yourself in trouble, every times

I have to bail you out and I will not do that again! Do you hear me? Yes but I was not the one that had the drugs and it was Johnny stash and not mine, well I still cannot help you and you need to called a lawyer and then you will not becoming back to here, do you hears me, but you the only family that I have and now you are kicking me out because of the drugs arrested? Yes because I am started a new life and I am going to make something out of my life and I am not going down, because of you and I wants to be successful and also not ended up prisoner again! When you gets bailed out you will have too move out and gets your own place, fine! Leo hung up the phone and said to Kelly, I don't need anymore problem and I just wants to lives straight lives and have a normal job and maybe someday open up my own restaurant that is my dreams, but you shouldn't been so hard on Leo, he is your younger brother and you need to understand that he is young and stupid and will make mistake and you did too, so I hope that you will go to him and help him out and let him be home with you, well I will think about it but I am not sure at this moment, and then Kelly said I need to go to my job and Joe said are still a exotic dancer and at the strip club? Yep it pays my rents and I somehow survive, well did you think about doing something else in life, well I am going to college and I wants to be a teacher and I am half ways there and went I am finished with college I will be teaching first grader and I didn't know that's! Well we didn't speak for month and you were dating Kelly, well don't reminder me, I won't! about half hour later Kelly got dressed up and gave Joe a kiss on his lips and said bye and slammed the door behind her and about two hour later, Jim went to the police station to pick up his brother and Joe said I will help you out but you cannot hang around with your buddy, well I won't and you have to promise me and then you can stay with me. I will be getting a job at a restaurant and I will be manger there and I just don't want any problem from you, even though I was in trouble before with the law. Yes Joe I will listens and behave what you says and do and I don't wants to be in prisoner and I will do and says what wants me and I will find a job and I will just stay out of trouble and that is promise,, okay! So Jim pays the bail and took Leo home and Leo when into his room and locked the door and when into the bathroom and lit a joint and got high and then Joe when into his room and lies down and thought about Kate and then he started to think about Kelly and about ten minutes later, Joe called Kate but her voice mail answers and Jim left a message,, would she like too meet up at the diner after the shift? And Jim fell asleep and Leo was playing the music and then fell asleep and the next morning he got a called from Kate and said sorry that I didn't calls you but my friend Candy, end up at the hospital with the overdose and I am with her alls night, and she will make it.

Maybe we can meet for lunch and I can make it for 1 pm is that fine?

Then they both hung up and later that day Leo just decided too sees his friends and once again he got high and really got crazy and beaten up a guy and they had to called for the ambulance and seems that guy will make it and Leo was in handcuff and taken to jail and Leo called Joe and he said what do you wants from me and now you are in big trouble and you will be in prisoner and I cannot help you, sorry! Joe hung up.

No Family ties

At the court Joe when to sees what will happen to his younger brother and he got five years and Joe walks out and never saws him again!

Jim move away from Manhattan and move too Florida and got a better job at a fancy restaurant and became a head manger and then he stay there for five years and then he open his own place in Florida and Joe was alone and didn't have know one at alls and just works hard and lost touch with Kelly.

One day Joe met Liza and she work with him and she was also in college but she wanted to be a nurse and but she was working has a waitress and had a little girl and Joe got along with her but they were only friend, and Liza invite him over her house but he refuse to go and but one night Jim decided to go to her, house and Joe went over and her little daughter greeting Jim and then they had dinner and then Liza daughter when on Jim lap and Jim told her a story and then Betsy when to sleep and Liza said you great with children, and well I did raise my brother and so that why? Well you never mention that you had one well I really don't want to talk about it.

"Then Liza got closer too Joe and he said I have too go and Liza said don't go stay with me and I am alone, well I told you that we are just friends and then Liza said fine! About ten minutes later, Liza ex husband came by and he started to swear and push her to the floor and Joe got up and said don't do that's and her and her Bill said what you are going to beaten me up and Joe said no I am just telling you…

Joe walks out and said I will calls you later and are sure that you will be fine? Yes I will be and I don't wants any trouble and Joe left and her ex husband Bill started to slapped her around and she fell and hurt her arm, and later that night the police arrives and told her ex to jail and Liza pressed charges and then later Liza called up to Joe and left the message that she was at the ER ands were be release until tomorrow.

Joe got the message and called her up and when to the hospital and took her home and then Liza settle and fell asleep and then Joe sat and watched them both and Joe slept on the chair in her bedroom and the next morning her took her daughter to school and Joe asked Betsy about her dad and she refuse too says anything, and then Betsy got to school and Jim said I will pick you up at 3pm and don't go with anyone I will be there! Betsy got out of the car and ran too her friends, and Joe left and when too sees how Liza was and then he knock at the door and Liza answers and said I will be there in one minute, but Joe had a bad feeling that Liza was not alone and so Liza came to the door and said I will be taking a nap so I will called you later, are you all right? Of course I am. And Joe left but had a gut feeling in his stomach, a d he when back and then Joe heard Liza screaming and Joe kick in the door and there was gun point at Liza and somehow Jim jump him and the gun fired and Joe didn't get hit but Bill did. Then about twenty minutes the police arrives and came inside and asked what happen and Liza explains that her ex husband tried to killed her and Jim save her, and then they took him out of the apartment and took him into the ambulance and he died and no charges were press, and Joe and Liza were Betsy got close, because of the incident and Joe told her about his past and Liza told him about her and how she was in prisoner for one year of armed robberies and theft and how her mom raise her daughter Betsy and how I change and promise I would not get into trouble again and I attended school and gets ahead, and I wants my daughter to have a better live than I did and he nodded his head and said I need to pick up Betsy and he was about to walks out of the door and he fell to the ground, and Liza tried to wake him up but he didn't move, and then she looked and he was shot in the stomach and Liza called the ambulance and they took him to the hospital and Liza called her neighbor to pick up Betsy at school.

Surgery

Liza left her house and headed to the hospital and too sees how Joe is and then called her mom and told her about the incident that Bill is dead and her friend is in the hospital that got shot by Bill by saving her and Liza said to her mom to check up on Betsy and her mom said I will comes over and Liza said you don't need too, but I will Liza, and Liza said I will talked with you later, that is fine. Liza arrive at the hospital Joe was in recovery and they did move the bullet and he will be fine and Liza was relief and waiting to sees Joe and Liza for hours and then about two hours later, Joe woke up and wanted too sees her and then Liza explains to Joe what happened and then he said "I thought I was not shot"? but you were and good that you collapse and I save you if you got my daughter and you probably were be an accident, well it is a blessing, I guess but I never been shot but it felt weird, well I just hope that you will be fine and you can stay at my house when you get release from the hospital and Joe said I wait and sees about that's!

Later that day, Joe laid on the bed and Liza was next too him and then her mom called and Betsy was asking for her and Liza said to Joe I need to go home because Betsy wants me and Joe said well go on I don't need a babysitter, and I will sees you later, and ok, so I will rest and we will be talking soon, yes! Liza left the hospital and she thought that she was being follows and now Liza was afraid and so Liza stop at the store to get some soda and sees if they follows her and then she got the soda and got into her car and drove a different ways home, and she called her mom too called the police and someone is follows her and Liza mom did called and about two hour later, Liza was home so was the Police car and the red car just pass her house, and Liza steps out and walks up too her door and her

14

daughter came to hug her and said, mommy are you okay? Liza nodded her head and said yes I am and they alls when inside and locked the door behind them.

Liza said too Betsy, why don't you do your homework and I will get dinner ready and Betsy when into her room and when on the internet and looked up some of things for her homeroom and then she spotted a man, scream out too her mom and her mom and her grandma ran inside her room and what did you sees well I saw that man with a black clothes and he was staring inside my room and Liza said I need to called the police to comes back and sees who that man is? Liza ma said know one that you know? Ma I did change since high school and since that my baby daughter was born and that was mistake with Betsy dad., but otherwise I think of my daughter first, and then they heard knock at the door and Liza said should I answers the door, no because you don't know who that person is? About ten minute later the police arrive and it was Bill younger brother Brad and he was yelling and screaming, you bitch you killed my brother with your new boyfriend and Liza told Betsy not too listen too that awful man and then police took Brad into custody and breach of peace and Brad was looking at Liza and saying I will get you and you are your family and you are going too pays,, and now Liza was afraid and didn't tried to shown it but her mom knew that she was really scare and told her mom. Maybe we should move away from Florida and her ma nodded her head yes! Before we do this I need to go and sees Joe and sees how he is doing but we need to pack tonight and so to New York too Manhattan and we do have relative living there? Uncle Tony and Uncle Tom will be the best place too moves, and they know how to protect us, good so we will need to calls them that we are coming, I will so I will tell Joe that we are going on vacation and then he will not except anything is strange, you are right, this is family business.

Liza left to sees Joe at the hospital and Joe was just lying on the bed and Liza walks in and he smiled and said I was thinking of you!!! That nice too hear and Liza smiled back at Joe and talks for awhile and left.

Left Town

L iza and her family left Florida and today Joe was getting release from the hospital and thought that Liza were comes by and sees him or take him home and no one show up and the nurse said " I guess your friends are on there ways" I don't know but I hope that they are here soon, but we cannot let you go alone, but I don't wants to stays, do you have any family in the area no I do not and so I think that you should go to a rehab until you complete recover, well I am fine and I will stay in bed and take my medications well but you be alone, then the nurse said I will let you stay at my place.

Are you sure about this? Yes I am and I live alone and I do work part time and I don't know your name well it is Rachel and I live here about one year and I came from Michigan and nice too meet you Rachel and Joe said well, hope that I will not be in your ways, and it will be all right with your husband and no I don't have a boyfriend, well I am just alone well you are saying too much information too me, well I trust you.

I am a stranger and no your not, I have been about a week and I started to know who you are! Okay, and then Joe said well I need some stuff from my place and were you get for me and I would give you my key to my place.

Well. I guess you trust me to go to your place and I know that we will get along fine, I hope and soon has I can take care of myself I will go, that is fine and I will have some company and it will be my pleasure.

Same here and Rachel , left Joe and when to his place and pick some shirts and pants and underwear and Rachel looked around and looked at his photo and she didn't sees any family photos and then took the stuff and left his place and when to her home and put the guest room and then when back to the hospital and Joe was saying well you a bit long and Rachel said I when home and drop your stuff and tomorrow you will be coming home with me and that is nice said Joe too Rachel,, and we can gets to know each others that nice. Meanwhile Liza and her family board the plane to New York and Uncle Tony will pick us up and Liza said I really likes Joe a lot and now I will never have a chance with him, I am sorry about that's but you were involve with Bill and Brad is a nut case and he were harms us and I think about moving is a good idea, I hope so. Hope that you are right, mom!

But Bill is dead and now Brad wants revenge and I think that New York city will be safer than here and I don't know if it is good for Betsy but she will make new friends and you will gets a job in a restaurant in Brooklyn and we will settle down and we will be happy and you don't go out to bar and pick up men like Bill, well I am just going to work and stay home, well you will follows my rules to stay alive, and what if I don't? you will end up dead and Brad will find you and he will, so how did he found us mom, well I didn't tell him but it seems like you did. Now you are calling me a liar and no I am telling the whole truth but you really got us on that flight quick and I don't know how you got the reservation and we are in Manhattan, and then we are taking the cab too Brooklyn to Uncle Tony, and we will get our own place and we will be fine, but mom I don't wants to lives with you and I am going to find my own place.

Right now you should not be seen or heard and then Liza said that was your whole not too live in Florida, and now you are saying, and you don't want to be alone, so mom what is going on? Well I am getting older and I thought that you were taking care of me and I would take care of Betsy when you are working but I still could have stay in Florida.

Well, you should have and now I am here and I don't have money to fly back to Florida and I am staying here mom for awhile when things cool off, fine and I am saying anything else, Liza walks out of the room and then Liza said well I am exhaust mom and so is Betsy.

Goodnight mom and Goodnight grandma, and walks out of the room.

Rachel and Joe

About five days ago, Joe got release from the hospital and Rachel , helped him out and asked him about his past and he was a little hesitate about talking about his past and then he started about himself and his brother were abuse by our parents and then we ended up at foster parents and then one night we ran off and kept running and then we were in trouble with the law and I was in the slammer for couple years and now my brother is in prison and he was having possession of drugs and assault and now he is serving five years and I just wants to be someone so I am working in a restaurant and then someday, and I will owe my own place and have all sorts of foods.

That is nice and you have a clean slat and now you are working hard and yes and I am staying out of trouble, and you are staying with me and that I really likes I don't like being alone. Yes but you should understand that we are only friends and I will be going back to Manhattan, and I will work near my old neighbor and I think that is a bad ideas and someone might have to gets even and then no I am not going my own ways and then you will be back in prison, and no, never I will never go back to that life again! stay with me, and I can make you happy, sorry I am in love with someone and I need to tell her, and we broke up about two years ago and I need her too hear the truth from me, but she might get you arrested for stalking her, but I need her to hear what I have to says and I need her to love me again! hope that she listened too you and I hope she forgive you, Joe and I didn't know before but I think that she will takes you back, I don't know if she will but she is one lucky, girl, hope that you will find her and tell her what in your heart, and but if she doesn't wants you and I will be yours!

Joe walks out and said I need some fresh air too think and I will be back soon!!! Joe walks and walks and thought about Kate and then Joe sat at the bench at the park and then he thought her saw her walking with a man.

Joe was about too get up but she was holding his hand and then Joe walks back to Rachel and gave her kiss and said what wrong? Joe said holds me and Joe said I will not lets you go!!! And then he carries her into the bedroom and they make love all night long!

The next morning, Joe got up and got dressed and took his stuff and when to his place and packed his stuff and make reservation to New York and meanwhile Rachel was in bed sleeping and then about one hour Later, Joe was on the flight and he didn't looks back and about one hour and half he was in Manhattan and he went to the bar and order vodka and tonic on the rocks. He had his suitcase with him and he just had one drink after another and then he when walking down the street and then stops at the building and walks inside and said, I need to rent a apartment and the landlord said don't I know you? Yes once I have lived her with my brother Leo, oh I see.

Then I do have a place on the fifth place and with two bedroom and Joe said that is fine and I will take it and she said you need to give me three month advance and that is no problem and then Joe signed the lease and walks into his new place and fell on the floor and then the next day! Joe woke up and said where I am? Then he looked out of the window and said I am home and now I will find Kate and need her too listens too me. Now Joe was getting a little paranoid about Kate and started to drink everyday and did go to work but he was not focusing on his live but on Kate.

Joe looks up Kate address and sends her red roses from anonymous, and Kate looks at the roses and thought who were send her them, and she thought it was Ted and she called him and said thanks for the roses and Ted said I didn't send them too you, and we should be just friends. And Kate said fine, and she hung up on Ted.

Kate thought that day and said who send them and I need to known.

The next day the phone rang and Kate answers and no one said nothing!

Rachel goes to Manhattan NY

Rachel booked a flight and came to New York to looks for Joe and Rachel said he make love and ran off and I need to find out why? Rachel came to New York and apply for job, has a RN Nurse and then Rachel stayed in the hotel for couple days and then find a place and near work and about two month later, Rachel hired a Private Investigate and too looks for Joe and I need to find him and I know that I am in love with him and I cannot let him gets in trouble because Kate and Rachel search for him but one thing that she know about Joe was that he wanted to own his own business like a restaurant and he were be working in that industrial and Rachel were know that she were find him, but meanwhile Joe was not working and just hanging out at his bar and Rachel was having a difficult it was taken that long too find him, but she told the PI to looked and didn't care how it were cost and then Rachel thought that she were looks around in the places that he told her, when he was in the hospital and but then Rachel was in the area and was really afraid, so Rachel when to work and met new friends and hang out with them and then one day she got a called from Ray and said I think that I have some good news about Joe and Rachel listens to him and she said I can go there and find him, and he said yes Rachel and that night she told her friends that let go to Star café and they asked why? But some of her friends refuse and she asked why? Well that is a bad place too go and why? Well first place it is a bad neighborhood and a lot of drug dealer and hookers, oh I sees, but I am still going maybe I will run into my old friend Joe, well called us went you get home, I will and so Rachel when with one of friend Tim and he was a tall and muscle and would know how to fight and wouldn't be afraid, and Rachel said to Tim thanks for coming along to Star café well I use too hang out there with my friend Leo and he when to prison for five years of possession and I turned my life around and I am clean, once upon times I was a addicted, and I when to rehab and I am not a junkie and I do have a good life and now I am getting marry soon and I do have a son, Andy and I am very happy to be a nurse and working that this hospital, and no one doesn't know the truth only you and I hope that you will not says anything to anybody, I promise too Tim. So it took about ten minutes to get there and then went they got inside and said I sees my buddy Joe and Rachel looks and it was her friend Joe and Tim and Rachel walks to him and he said what are you doing here to Rachel? Well I move from Florida to New York and so why did you runs off that night and didn't even tell me, and I was worry about you, well it is a long story and Rachel said I am not going anywhere and then they spoke for hours and hours and Tim said I have too go, my girlfriend will wandering where am and Joe and Tim said it is good to sees you man!!!

Later that night Rachel and Joe talks and talks and then Rachel said I got to go and hope that we keeps in touch and I do have a early shift so talks with you soon and Rachel walk out of the bar and tag a cab and went home and then Joe thought and said well I don't have Kate, maybe I should sees Rachel and later that night Joe got up and left the bar and when home and the next morning he search for work and clean up and started to think positive and thought about his life and if Kate not in it and he will be fine too, and so he send a lot of resumes and move out of the bad area and move upper Manhattan and then got a job at a fancy restaurant and called up Rachel and then they started to sees each others and then Joe move in with Rachel and Joe when too work and Rachel stay home and they both talks about married and Joe was in live with Rachel and but Rachel was not sure that he was really in love with her and so she said we are moving too fast, and what do you mean? We just got together and now you want to marry me?

Joe and Rachel Wedding day!

About ten month later, Joe and Rachel wed at St Martin Church and Rachel had her family from Michigan to comes and then they had the reception at a fancy restaurant and then they danced and had the wedding cake and then they ate and then they left for their honeymoon and Kate was standing in the back of the room and when Rachel and Joe left to go on there honeymoon, they kicked out Kate and said you crash a wedding and gets out and we don't wants too called the police and then Rachel dad what is the emotion here, so woman came here and He said hope that you chase her away! On the way to the airport, Rachel was a little quiet and Joe asked why are so quiet and Rachel said this happened so fast and maybe it is a mistake that we got marry, what? You love me and I love you and how can it be a mistake, you still love Kate, I told y0u that is over a long time and I love you, and be happy, Rachel, I am happy, went I came to New York to looks for you I didn't think that I were be your wife, well that how things works out and now are going on ours honeymoon to Hawaii and that is true and he were love me and I love you and they kissed all the ways and then they got at the airport and Rachel spotted a woman and but nothing about it and they got there board pass and they got the plane and so did Kate in first class, and Joe and Kate were kissing and holding hands and then Rachel fell asleep and Joe asked if he can have a vodka and tonic on the rocks and then he gave a few drinks and then he spotted Kate, and he rubbed his eyes and couldn't believe that it was Kate.

Suddenly Joe got up from his seat and tried to enter first class but he was told that he was not allows and sat back and now starting to think about Kate the love of his life and now he was a bit nasty to Rachel and then Rachel said what wrong? Nothing, I know that you are lying and stop it, fine I saw Kate on this flight in first class so you don't wants to b e with me and just with her is that right? No I love you but you are in love with Kate and if you wants a divorce, I will give it too you, no I wants to be with you and I just wants to know why she is on this flight.

But Joe got up and looking around and sees if he could sees her and then he saw her sitting to man, and walks back to the seat and Rachel said what wrong nothing, you are not telling me, so what did you sees, well I saw Kate, what? Your ex is on this flight, yes and you didn't want telling me, I don't want no secrets between us, I won't! Then Rachel got up and she was about to walks up to Kate and Joe said don't, your not stopping me, yes I am. Joe got up walks up to Rachel what are you doing? Well I am stretching my legs, I think you are lying, this is our honeymoon and your ex is causing trouble, well I didn't tell her I have not seen over two years.

So Rachel went back to seat and Joe sat down and then spoke that don't even says hi too her, unless she said, I don't even speak too her if you want be marry too me, do you hear that now your threaten me? No, I am not but if you do it over, we got marry and now you threaten with a divorce, first day married, and you don't believe me, I will. Joe got up and left Rachel at the seat, where are you going? Nowhere, you are going too see that bitch, but I am not. Just getting vodka and tonic, well I want a coke and rum.

I will be back , good I need a drink , be back I will and five minutes Kate approach Rachel and said I saw you with a man, and I think that I knew him, and Rachel said, yes my husband Joe. Well did you meet him, that is none of business, and Rachel got up and leaves us alone. Then Joe came back with drinks and leaves us alone, go back, and bother us.

Then Kate went back, was mad and furious, and knocks a drink near her seat and starting screams and yelled at everyone. About five minutes they would go to landing in Hawaii…they waiting and then got off walks to the gate toward the terminal and went too gets there bags, and took the cab and when to there hotel and they headed outrigger hotel .

Is it far but it is so beautiful here it is like paradise, I sees the pacific ocean and sees diamond head, so are going takes the tourist to the pineapple factory and gets some pineapple ice cream, but first we need to check in, I agree and we should take a walks on the beach later, yes!

When they check in and went into the room and put the bags on the locks the door and just lies on the bed and fell asleep.

Next morning Rachel got up and woke Joe and said so what are we going to do? Relax in bed, but it is a beautiful day and I want to be at the beach and get some tan, Joe said fine we will go out and dip in the ocean, and then we will spend some time in the room, fine! I will meet up at the beach, I need to check and calls the restaurant and sees how it doing? Fine, I will sees in ten minutes, good. So Rachel took a blanket and walks on the beach, and she couldn't believe that Kate was lying on the blanket, and Rachel said what fuck are you are doing here? Well I am on vacation and Kate and you are staying in the same hotel? Well you mean the "outrigger "? Yes but why? I am going after your husband I am seeing someone and I am love, but seems like you are after Joe, no you are but you paranoid no I am not. Then Joe walks toward the beach and saw Rachel and Kate argument with each others, and Joe steps in and said what fuck is she doing here? Kate spoke you are fucking bastard that swindle peoples and ended up in the slammer. Joe and Rachel asked Joe is that truth? Answered yes I did but I am not the same man, and what else? Assault and battery, then she walks away, Joe called to Rachel lets me explained, I don't wants too talks right now, leaves me alone, and then Joe walks back to Kate, now are happy?

Leave me alone, I still have restrain order but that long time and why do have this grudge, I did steal your money, I loved you, just lies. Then Joe walks back too the hotel, and find Rachel, he looked for her and Rachel said everyone make mistake I was wrong, and Joe and Rachel , and I love you and I do trust you, and I feel the same, and walks back to the hotel and went inside the room and that day they make love. The phone offs the hook and they stay in the hotel room, and had room service and stay days in bed.

But we are hiding out and I don't wants too sees the sights and I wants sail on a boat and I wants to go the " north shore" and feed the fish, we will but I wants quality time with you, and promise that you will not leaves me? I cannot, but why I just can't, you are being honest. Thanks being that!

Rachel got up from the bed and got dressed and said come on Joe, I am ready to go, fine, then Joe got dressed and they left the room and took the elevator down and got off the elevator and when into the lobby.

Take tours of island and Rachel said why we go and sees the Arizona don't and then Lau and eat some pigs that were smoke in the ground, that sound good. Maybe tomorrow we can go the north shore and that is a good idea, and sail on the boat and sees the island, and then sees the falls and beautiful flowers, but especially feeding the fishes. They sat on the bus and looks out of window and seeing the beautiful view, and Joe was holding her hands and kissing her tender lips, and the tour they went to the restaurant to have dinner, and Rachel said looks at the ships sails at night. They are so beautiful and then Joe order dinner for of them and then Kate enter the restaurant and Rachel, said what is bitch following us here? Joe gets up and walks toward her and then Kate called security, then Joe walks back and we cannot stay here, this bitch is ruining ours honeymoon, you are right Joe. Rachel said I am not hungry, just left leaves the restaurant now!! I cannot take it, okay I will tell the waitress to pack it up into the box and we will eat in our room, good!

They both left and Kate staring went they left the restaurant and left.

Left Hawaii on the earlier flight

The next morning Joe and Rachel took the flight and looked around she was not on the flight and they both were relief.

So Joe kissed Rachel said "I love you" and I love you too.

On the plane they kept alls the ways home and then they woke up when they landed at Kennedy airport and Joe said wake up sleeping head, and Rachel and then he kissed her and said, I cannot wait too sees ours new home and it will be great and you can make it the ways that you like it and I will honey and I will decorate the whole place but first our bedroom and then the rest of the house and then two minutes later, Rachel mom called and said, are you still in Hawaii? No we are at the airport at Kennedy and we will be heading home soon, so I will called you later, fine mom and then she hung up the phone and Joe said what she wanted too sees how we were and if we were still in Hawaii and I didn't tell her that we left early because your ex girlfriend, but I need apology and I thought that she were not stalk us but I thought didn't even wanted too sees me, well what wrong with her? I don't know and I don't care and I am in love with you and that's alls it should count, you are right and I hope that she doesn't find out where we lives. I don't think so because I put the deed in your maiden name and she will not trace it, good, but also we need to make sure that somehow she does not find out where you own your restaurant and don't cause any trouble.

I hope not Rachel but I was very young and I just thought by hiding the past from Kate, and it just backfire and then they accuse me that I was stalking her but I didn't. so what is the truth and but they didn't believe me and so that moment Kate broke up with me and then I just walks out but they said I was the one looking through the window and I did get lock up and promise not too sees her again!

Then I left and the next day, I got a restrain order and I didn't see Kate again! This whole story, I met Kate online and we met for coffee and it was love at first sight and the parents were against me and so it ended.

You have nothing too worry about Rachel, are you should and you don't you have any feeling for her, no don't you know how I feel about you, are so unsecured, about Kate and you are my wife and I love with my whole heart and you means so much too me, well I don't know what do you means? Then Joe said, I will unpack after I come back from the restaurant, and Rachel said well I have called into the hospital and tell them that I am back, and I will be coming too, work on Monday! So I check your schedule Rachel and I will gets back soon with you, that fine today I will rest and if I am needed at the hospital called me, fine! Then she hung up the phone and sat on the couch and looked around and then Joe came in and said everything is fine at the restaurant and so we can have a relaxing night and Rachel said that is great and so what should I make for dinner well I will order a pizza and we will have a glass of red wine, that sound good, honey! So Joe got up and then order the pizza and put on some soft music and they started to dance and then the phone rang and Joe answered and no one at the other end and then he hung up and once again the phone rang and then Joe answered and no one and then it was his brother Leo and how did you gets this number, well I called information and I told you that we are not brother anymore, and then Leo said well, we are brother and I do need you and I will be getting out prison and I need a place too stayed, well you cannot stay with me, but I will be homeless and they will not releases me, unless you says yes!!! Sorry I need to says, please let me stay I promise I will not cause any trouble, Joe, I heard that before but I think about it and I will get back too you tomorrow, and Joe explained to Rachel that his brother will be coming out a prison and need a place too stayed.

Joe and Rachel talks about Leo and Rachel said that fine and she said yes he can stay but if cause troubles he will be out of here do you hear that? Yes, and I just wants to just hang out when we are at work and I wants him too works and then he can pays his share until he gets his own place, Joe,, yes I do understand complete, and they both agree, about Leo.

About five days later, and Leo got release from prison and then came to live with Rachel and Joe in the guest bedroom and then Leo was just a lazy con man that wanted money from his brother and Joe refuse and told him that he can stay for few days and then he needed to find his own place and work and if he doesn't, wants do that's but you need to do that's! I have change my life and so can you, Leo, and then Leo mention that some woman came to prison visit him and Joe said how did she looked, well very hot and sexy and then Leo said it was Kate, and she still love you, stops this I am marry too Rachel, and then he walks into his room and lied down on the bed. Joe and Rachel talked about Kate and what does she wants from you I don't know and she didn't know where you live? What you saying that Leo told her, and then the phone rang and it was the hospital and they are short handed, well I will sees you later… Rachel got ready and got her stuff and then left the house and when too the car and then when too work and meanwhile Joe was sitting alone and then Leo, got up and then went inside the room and said where is Rachel and she when too work and I will be going back in two hours and you can make something too eat, well I am not hungry and Joe left the house and then Leo called Kate and said I am in the house and I will give you direction,, and Kate said I know where you are, and I don't need to be there tonight and they will not figure out that you told me, Leo said if they figure out that I told you they will kick me out and I will be homeless and what then? I don't know I will get you a place too stayed.

You promise and no one will get hurt, no one I promise! Take my word

Leo move out stalk by Kate

Leo move to upper Manhattan and Joe is trying too figuring out, where he got the money and Leo got a job at an office and working for a big shot. And his duty at duty likes making appointment, and having meeting and giving prices and order, Joe was surprise about achieve and getting out trouble.

Rachel said what the wrong is, that he suddenly moves out, I don't know.

Joe said don't looks for trouble, I am not! Then Joe said I need to go to work and Rachel, fine, and I will be late, so I will wait up for you…

No, you don't have and then the phone rang, and Rachel answered and no one on the line and Rachel hung up. Then Rachel decided to take shower and left the cell, and then Leo snuck in and looks at the mail and stole a letter, and looks around and snuck out… Then Rachel step out of shower and wiping her body and breast gentle and then put some bikini panties, and then put on the pajamas, then went into bed and then got out bed and check, out the door and the door lock and went to the bedroom and went to bed, and turn off. About three hours later, Joe came in very quietly and put on the light in the living room and then he check the mail and nothing important and then when into the bedroom and got undress and when into the bed and Rachel was fast asleep, and then Joe fell asleep and then the phone rang and he answered and no one said a word and he said what the hell do you wants from me, and then she spoke, I wants to see you and Joe said it is too late, and you did accuse me has stalker, and I never did, leaves me alone, it was not my fault it was my parents, that made me break up with you, but you should have told me, and we probably be marry now and not you with Rachel, well I guess that how life works out and I am very happy with her and please leaves me alone and my wife, no I need to sees you!! No I will not, I will comes too your restaurant tomorrow for dinner, don't comes.

Then she hung up the phone and Joe fell asleep and then Rachel woke up and said who called? Just a wrong number! Your not lying too me? No of course, and not keeping secrets, I do understand, Rachel, I will be totally honest with you, I hope you are, and I will always tells you what on my mind, good, so then he put his arms around her and hold her tight and then her cell rang and then she answered and it was the hospital and they needed her too comes too works and Joe said you just came home and you have too go back? Yes I do and I sees you later at the restaurant and Joe said you don't have too, and Meanwhile Leo and Kate were planning to get Joe alone with her and somehow Keeps Rachel away and Leo said what is the plan, well one of my friend works in the hospital just called Rachel and she is on her ways and then I will called Joe and tell him that I wants to meet him at the coffee shop on the corner, and so I will not make the called you will and then he will comes and meet you, then he will know that we are working together, well you will be there and then I will walk in and then you make a excuse and then you leaves, that sound good! So Leo and Joe meet up at the coffee shop and they talked for awhile and then Kate walks in and said, well what a small world and then Joe said too Leo was this a set up, I don't know what you are saying, and I did wants to talked to you about a money matter and I don't even know who this chick is?

But Joe was a bit suspicious about Leo, and Leo got up and kick down the chair and said I will called you later and you are leaving me with her alone, okay! You wants me too stay I will, no just go and we will talked later.

Joe was so furious that he almost knock down a plate on the floor and then his cell when off and it was Rachel and Joe didn't answered it and it went to voice mail and Rachel left a message where are you, I thought you were in bed and your not here? So went you get this message called me, right now!! But Joe said I cannot be here with you I have a wife and I love her very much and you did hurt me and broke my heart and didn't let me explained about my past and so you just listened to your mom and dad and left me out in the cold and also you put a restrained order and I just left town and I move on and then I got into trouble and then I ended up in the hospital where I met Rachel and then I ran back too New York and left Rachel because I didn't wanted my heart to break again! So Rachel follows me and now I am back home and I am very happy with my wife and then you follows us too Hawaii and then now you are here and so what do you wants from me? Well I just wants too have a chance too explained that I still love you, but been over a long time and I thought you move on and so leave me alone, I will one thing you need to tell me that you don't love me, looks into my eyes and tells me, so Joe was looking into her eyes and said I can't! Then Kate said you still love me? Yes I never stop but I am not available to be with you. You need to tell Rachel that you don't love her; I am not going too break her heart because I love you, and you are crazy. Stops this need too end and I just wants to says bye and we will not sees each others again, promise that you will not called me or watched me, I cannot I love you, Joe and I will never stop loving you!!!!

I need to go home now and don't call me again! Why are you acting this ways, I know that you feel the same about me has I feel about you! Don't hold back meet me at the place and we can talked, no I am going and don't contact me, I will put a restrain order on you, no you will not and your brother will suffer the conquers if you do, I will make a lot trouble for you and Leo take my word. Well his great job will be getting fired and he will end up in trouble and prison, you are threatening me? No but warning you, well I don't likes threaten from anyone and he left the coffee shop and then when home and called Rachel that he is on his ways home and Rachel said where did you go for a walks? Just around the block.

Joe and Rachel the Halloween Party

Joe walks inside the building and then took the elevator to the top floor and when inside and Rachel was waiting for him too comes in…

Joe came in and Rachel said where were you I thought you were in bed and then Joe explained that he met up with Leo and Leo had a problem and needed too talked with him but he didn't mention anything about Kate.

Then Rachel said we are going too have a Halloween party and I did invite some of my friends from the hospital and we will have fun and you can invite yours, fine! About two weeks later I am going too visit my mom and dad and were you like to comes and Joe said I cannot leaves the restaurant so I will stay home, is that okay? Sure I will catch up with them and I do have time off from the hospital and that you didn't tell me until now, well I just decided too do that's! That is fine, but the next visit I will go with you but now it is a bit difficult with the restaurant with the new employees, I do understand and no secrets or lies, no I am telling you the truth…

Well we will have about fifty guest and we need to dress up in costume and then we will have music and wines and whiskey and will also buy the vodka and that is good and I don't like the ordinary whiskey and I will invite Leo and I will need to talked to him about the matter that he when behind my back but now he had change but I didn't like how he did things,, I don't understand, why he helped out someone that broke my heart and now he is working at the company that she own and he is very happy about that's!

I am not going to ruin his life and Rachel said I don't know what you are saying about Leo, well it is a long story but not now so we are planning a party and you will be going away for a week, I just wants too be close too you and hold you tight, you will! Later that night Rachel had to go to work and Rachel said I make some beef stew and it is on the oven and you just have too heat it up and you can share it with Leo, well Leo is not too crazy about beef stew, well you can asked, I will and then she ready for work and then Joe just sat and thought about Kate. Then he thought should I invite her to the party and then he said too himself I will think about it, and Halloween was about in three days and he needed to add her name but then Leo said she is out of town and she is visiting her brother and she will be back on the November 3 and then you can called her, thanks for telling but why did you set me up that night? Well if I didn't she was going to fired me and I needed that job, and I did meet a nice girl and her name is Liza and she has a ten year old daughter and I think I love her.

So where did you meet her, well working at a pizza joint in Brooklyn at her uncle place and she is very pretty and nice and I like her and I don't wants you too ruined it for me, why? I won't say anything too her and she are welcome and can her daughter Betsy comes along? What? You said Betsy, I think I know her, don't says that's! then Joe said well bring her, and then he said thanks, and she need too meet new peoples, and she will likes you, I hope not I am a marry man, I don't means it that ways!

So be here on Monday at 7pm and the party started dress up costume and you need to bring something beside a date because it pot luck, okay!

Then Leo left and when downstairs some of his friends from the past shown up and Leo said I am not the same and I do have a job and I don't need to get into trouble and I also serve my time and I was not one that had the drug but I was the fall guy and I spend five years and now you just go and leave me alone, no you know too much about his and Leo said I will not says a word and I have not and why are you going after me, I don't do drugs or steal from the rich, and they were about too beat him up and Joe came down on the right times and save his little brother and then Joe called the police and they arrives and took them away.

Leo said thanks Joe for saving my life and then they when back into Joe place and they discuss that he need too press charges, and Leo refuse, they will killed me!!! I will not press charges and they will walks and they will comes back and beat you too death, don't scare me, Joe I am afraid and I need to be quiet about the whole incident, but why? I don't wants you involve but I am all ready, sorry! About ten minutes later, Leo left and Joe locked the door behind him and then Leo when into his car and drove off and then Joe was very worry about Leo. And later that night, Joe called

Leo and he didn't answered and now he was getting worry and about two hours later, Rachel came home and then said what wrong? So I think that Leo is in trouble with his old friends and they wanted to beat him up and Rachel said what? He will be bringing trouble here and I don't wants him here and Joe said this is my house too and Leo is welcome,, so I will not accept this do you understand, Joe., yes but it will be okay! Then Joe kissed Rachel and then he pick her up and carried her to the bed and then lay her on the bed and kept on kissing, and then the phone rang and Rachel said don't answered it, and then Joe said I need too sees, well fine.

Joe looked and it was a wrong number and then when back too Rachel and then they kiss and kiss and they make love and then they make love all night and then Joe got up and then went into the shower, and then Rachel join him and they make love in the shower and then Joe got out and Rachel stay in and then Joe wipe her body from top too bottom and then pick her up and make love on the floor and Rachel was moaning and groaning and then they Joe hold her and they fell asleep and then the next morning!

Joe got up but it was early and Joe needed to place order for his restaurant and Rachel headed to work and said I will sees you later and I probably had a double shift and I will called you if I do.

Joe said that fine and I will be going to work myself and I will see you!

Halloween October 31,

Tonight is "Halloween Night it is October 31, and there will be a party at Joe and Rachel house and about fifty guests.

That night the snow started to snow and Rachel, said hope ours guests, all will comes in this weather, but then they arrives, Rachel take out the foods and music and some were with mask, and they started dancing and talking and Rachel, mingle with the guest, Joe started to talked with Liza and Leo, and Rachel didn't like Liza and then Liza and Rachel when into the others the room, and said why did you comes and are you after Joe, no I am in love with Leo and you have no reason too be jealousy and Leo love me and my daughter and we are going too get married and so I think that you got close and because you wants Joe, no!! I am in Love with Leo and I will be your sister law, and you will tried to gets close to my husband and you are accusing me for no apparent reason, then Leo came and said we are not staying, Joe because your wife is crazy, and Leo and Liza left and then Joe yelled at Rachel, I am sorry but I wants too be close to my brother,, and now you chase him away, but why are you so possession. I hate you how you behave of our guest and then Joe walks out of the house and Rachel said where are you going? Then slams the door behind us and Rachel said don't go and I don't wants to be embarrass, one of her guest asked where did your husband when? He when too buy more scotch and whisky and vodka, oh he didn't leaves the party because of arguing with your new sister law too be, so you were a busy body and listens too what I was saying too Liza and then her friend said I am not going too stick my nose but you are making trouble and you need to be calm and relax and tell him how you feels about the past relationships,, well it is difficult and he does have a colorful past so I am just being his wife and I don't wants any slut inference in my life.

So you are doing in the wrong ways! I know what I am doing!

Soon has they walks out the lights went out and Rachel and Joe and Liza said what happened here, I don't know but the city is dark and we should gets out of the dark but I don't have any flashlights and I don't sees anything and it is alls your fault, Liza by chasing after my husband and now I am paying the price and now I am stuck inside and in the cold and the dark, and then Liza said you didn't have too follows us but you did.

Then Joes said to Rachel we will be fine honey, and now you are calling me honey when your mistress is here, no she doesn't means anything too me and then Rachel said I am not staying here. Yes you are no I am not!!!

Rachel said I am going back home and I am not staying and you are not going too force me…. No your not!!! Don't be stubborn, I am not! I don't want to be here with you and your lover, I told you it is over, when I came? No I love you, and I really do, Really Rachel. Rachel walk into the building and Joe follows her and Liza got pissed and Rachel walks up the stairs and Joe was behind her and said wait for me, no go too that slut.

Then Leo came up too Liza I know all the long he was your lover and now Rachel known and you were not in love with me but with my brother that why you wanted too get marry too me that is not true and I love you. Leo said too Liza all the times that you wanted to gets close too me but you wanted to get close too Joe, but why? I left him but I loved him and my mom force me to leaves Florida and Joe. otherwise I would been married too him and not you, so Rachel said I know that you were not in love with Leo. Rachel said to Joe why didn't you tell me that truth about Liza that you were in Love with her and not with me, I would have understand and I wouldn't marry you and now I am going too have your baby and so I think that we should get an divorce, no I wants too be with you, I don't wants your lies…Still climbing the stairs and then Rachel almost fell down and said I cannot looks at you right now!!!

I think that I might gets a abortion no you cannot do that's yes I can do it and it is my body and you have nothing too says! Still the lights didn't come on and I wander what happened? And I don't know. But I think it is the snow storm, and that effective by the storm. What are we doing do? I don't know but I am not going too be stuck with you the stairway with you, but let me explains, I don't know listens, but you need too, no you will tells me lies… Joe said I want you too keep the baby, I don't wants this baby and

I want you...leaves me alone and they kept walking and then they heard a boom and what was that's I don't know I hears that sounds like someone broke in.. Who I don't know but we should gets inside and should be safe and not in danger. Comes on hurried and I don't like it...

They would near the apartment and they heard peoples yelling and screaming and then they got inside and locked. Rachel said to Joe and there guest were eating and drinking...Joe what going on I need to put on the news but our electricity is out.. And don't you have a battery radio; I do so get the radio. Joe went into the room and looks out of the window and was terrified what he was seeing and didn't say anything to Rachel. But kept to him, and I need to be silent and not scare any of my guest. Got the radio and walks out of room and put on radio and sat down and listens and then Rachel sat down and said what wrong? Nothing! I see in your face, so you are a liar about you; you find investigate to find me and stalk.

So you are calling your wife a stalker but I loved you and you felt the same, at one time. Yes but I don't know but I need time too think, said Joe but now let just worried that we should be fine, after the storm that things will be normal and agree, and the guests and what going on? I don't know but we are fine. Then the guests started too panicked.

Joe and Rachel hold on tight, and Rachel just let go went into the bedroom.

Day one lights out

Alls the guests snuggle together, and had candles and lanterns and flashlights and the party was over and it was cold and chilly, ands fireplace was on, Joe said I can gets a drinks and the guests nodded and said we are fine. Later Rachel said ,there is on the table and one of the guest, we just wants to go home but now you need to stayed, but ours children will be frighten, so why don't just call home, I will. So she pick up the phone, and the line was dead, and she panic and worry. Then she sat next to Joe and started too talked with him, and tried too not make worry mores.

Later that night they thought the lights would going too be on, so they flicker and it was pitch black and sat very quietly. Then Joe put on the radio and there was a SPECAIL REPORT that everyone too stayed inside. So what does it means? I don't know but be quiet, I do wants too listens to the rest of report, okay we will be. Then there was a warning, one of guest I am going home, no you are staying, ands about ten minutes later Leo and Liza and Rachel what is she doing here, and you believe what that bitch is saying? Yes she is my fiancée, and I am going married Leo. So come on in and sit down and Joe was furious at Rachel and said I need to talked too you now, we have situation and we need too settle it now. We are not going nowhere so let go into the bedroom and Rachel said not now, we have company, fine, you just comes up with excuses. Leo said Liza do you really love me? Yes I do and you don't have too asked. About half hour later they heard planes and helicopters above the buildings and then they heard shooting and did you hears that's? Yes this is really shit going on, yes it is and we need too stay inside, it could be epidemic, what you are saying I don't know but we will be all right! You are so positive, you are Joe, yes.

So listens to the headline on the radio, some kind of spill and something is spreading, but what? I don't know.

They alls sat quietly in the living room, and then they heard a knock at the door and Joe got up and lookout of the peek hole and didn't recognized. I am not letting them in and I don't know them and they looked very strange, please Joe don't let them in and gets way from the door, I am and they are banged it and trying too gets inside. What those peoples wants from us, I don't know but, they must be hurt and we should help them and we don't know what wrong with them...that is true, and I am not willing too take any chances, do you understand what I am saying Joe? Yes loud and clear, good, and locked the door tight and stay away from the door...let be silent and quiet and don't let them hears you, okay! About two hours later they were gone and Rachel and Joe were relief that those strange peoples are not around and Leo and Liza said I have too take Liza home too her daughter and her mom,, you are not going, they are waiting for anyone too comes out. I think they are infection and I don't know what they have and I don't wants too get it, so you are not going, so called them, you know the phone is not working, but you are not stepping out of this place, fine! But I am worry about my mom an d my daughter Betsy, and then Rachel said you should have stayed home with them and I just wanted too meet you and I knew it was Joe and I didn't wants to cost any problem but you did.

Then Rachel said are you still going too married Liza? Of course I am. Are you insane and she is in love with Joe and she is using you, stops saying that Rachel, okay, so let her leave, no not alone but I am going with her and you are willing too risk your life for her that she doesn't love you, why are being such of bitch, and then Liza got her coat and then Leo got his coat and then when to the door and said bye too his friends and then Rachel said Leo is not really your brother but Kate? That is true and I didn't wants too lies too you but you did. Rachel got furious and said go with them and I don't wants too sees your face again!

Day two lights out

J oe and Liza and Leo walks out of the apartment and Leo said you can go back too Rachel but Joe said, I am going with you guys if you don't mind.

" then Joe said get into my car and I will drive you too your home, well we can walks and it will be fine, no it could be dangerous out there, we are willing too take our chances. Are you sure? That you will drive us too Long Island and then you will go back too your wife Rachel, good and then I will stay for a while if it ok with you. No I will stay with you and Leo that is not a good idea., but why because I still have strong feeling for you, but why are you telling me that when Leo is sitting next too you and you are hurting him and don't you realize what you have done destroy my married and now you are hurting ,my best friend and we are trying to get too your daughter and mom and you are trying too kiss me and hold me in front of him, don't know that I never felt nothing for you but only sex.

You are lying too me and don't denied yourself what you feel for me and my daughter I just been nice and that how you are paying me back, I lost my wife and my baby and I will not be able too sees them again because of you, don't accuse me, why you are so innocent? No but I couldn't explains why I left, well you should told me and I was stranded in the hospital and Rachel got me back to health and you didn't even called me.

Then I didn't have no place too go and Rachel took me to her place and then I heal and I when back too Manhattan and then she somehow follow me and then we got married and now we are except a baby and she doesn't wants me because of you, well you should have told her that once you were in love with me, I was never in love with you but I was lonely and you were there and I think that you should married Leo, and then

Leo said I don't wants her, because she Liza didn't love me and I am just going for a ride and take her too her mom and her daughter then I am leaving so am I .

Meanwhile they were on the highway and it was pitch black and then Joe said look up it is the "moon eclipse " and I think that is causing some kind of weird effective on the peoples., you can be right , and I think we should just keeps on going and we should be fine. I agree with you Joe. But Liza was really pissed with Joe and Leo and didn't speak to them until they reach her mom house, and then they stop and it was really peaceful and quiet and Liza said I really don't like it and I am very scare, and then a moment later, Liza said, looks the door is wipe open, and Liza was about too run

inside, Joe stops her, don't run inside, I have a bad feeling so do I. Liza steps inside and everything was on the floor and no one around and Liza called out "Betsy" ands nothing and I shouldn't have not left them here alone and I am worried sick about them we need to find them now, and about one minute later, Betsy came out of the corner and said MOMMY! And Liza said where grandma? They took her out of the house and they were ugly peoples and I hid in the corner and they didn't sees me and they were drool from there mouth and they were like not alive.

"What do you means, Betsy? Well they were ugly looking peoples and they were like walking in a limp and they were like in the funeral home, you are saying they were like dead? Yes, and very scaring and I ran and hid and I tried to help her but they pull her into the street and I just ran away and hid in the corner and they follow me in but they couldn't find me so, was very quiet and don't make a sound they will hears you, who will?

Then Joe said to Leo we should go inside, because I think they are out here! And they are not like us, I don't understand what you are saying Joe.

Okay, I think that we are dealing with the undead and they wants too eat ours brains, are you saying "Zombie"? Yes!

How do we kill them? Shoot right in the brain.

Day three lights out

J oe and Leo got inside with Betsy and Liza and Joe said do you have any weapons in this house? No! I don't and Betsy said I am so, so scare that they will comes and get me and I will walk with them, no I will protection my dear daughter. Then Liza asked who will comes those ugly looking peoples that eat the flesh and then Liza said don't hear what she is saying, well not sure but she does have a good imagination and I think she is just telling us a story but you have seen them, yes I have but they are only sick, well they tried too catch us, that is true, but that doesn't means that they are zombie, I didn't says that's yes you did apply they are.

Maybe I did and I think that are just cold and hungry and they don't have no place too stay and they just wander on the street, that is your conclusion, yes it is and what wrong with that maybe we should invite them inside are you nuts? No I am not but I feel that you should help peoples in trouble and they might end up eating you up, that is ridicules and you are willing put your daughter in danger? No, so be quiet. I am trying too be but I am terrify about this situation and I just wants to make it alive and I wants my daughter too sees her grandma and not like a undead creature.

But at this point I don't know what going on but I just wants too see my mom and I wants be home with lights and coking dinner.

I just want things to be like they were before and not likes this they are now and we don't even know if it is an epidemic, or it is only the cold that is effective peoples, well we don't have answers. But times when by and it still was cold and no heat or lights and I thought we were died, not because the creature but the cold and being hungry and unable too eats.

But Betsy said to me that we will be okay, there is dry foods that we are able too eat but we need to be hidden and not make a sound.

Do you understand said Betsy too her mom and the friends in the house.

But Leo was walking back and forward he wanted to go out and gets some help and he felt that he was stranded and probably were died. But Joe said stops thinking negative about this and we will make it alive and we need to block the doors and windows and keeps them out, do you understand not to attempt to steps out, so make you make you boss, I need to find my family and I need to find Kate. But I hope that she is safe but I need to go and find her, you will make us a target if you step outside and we will wait until morning and we will leave this place and find your family.

Just be patience and :Leo, and Liza said I will tried my cell phone and reach someone that can helped us, but don't attract attention, okay I won't!

Leo and Joe and Betsy and Liza sat in the dark and they heard sound like moaning and then they heard a big bang and then Leo said I think that I heard someone trying opening the door, and now they were getting worry and scare what might happen yet! They are getting in, we need to stop them they will eat us up, I will you protection, I honest you from the bottom of my heart and I didn't love Rachel and it was always you!!! How can you says that too Liza, I am in love with her and you buddy are in love with Kate and now you are saying that you love Liza? Right now and I don't like what going too happened so I need to tell her now I feel. I have a feeling that they are going too break in and they will grab Betsy and me and then you guys and then we will be dead meat, stops saying that's we don't know if they are zombies, that is true and we don't know what we are dealing with and we don't have weapons to protection, we are goner, stops this negative talking I don't wants to hears that's! Then Joe and Liza walks in the bedroom and Joe said I wants to make love too you about Leo.

Leo said wait a minute I am not going to be a babysitter too your daughter when you are having sex with that man and I will be watching your daughter, no I will not and I am going out of here, are you crazy.

Day four lights are out

Leo was going to step out and Betsy follows him and Leo said go back to your mom and Joe and Betsy said no I wants too sees Grandma, your mom going too killed me that I took you, so I am going back inside, can we go now, to find grandma, no we are going inside and then they started too comes closer and then Liza called out too Leo and said where is Betsy and didn't says anything and then Liza came out of the room and the door was open and then Liza scream and said they are gone and then Joe ran into the room.

About one minute later they came from the outside into the indoor and what are you trying to hurt me and have a heart attack. well I am sorry but Betsy follows me and now they know that we are inside and they will try too get inside of you how could you put us in danger. I just wanted to go home and sees if Kate and my family and your brat follow me, don't called her names, so if you wants too go just leaves, and he took his bag and hug Betsy and said I will be fine, and Betsy said how could you let him go, I loved him and you are with this man and I don't even know him, but you will honey and he is very friendly man and he love children, I think that is a phony, stop this., fine. Leo walks toward the car and it was clear and he drove off and they didn't sees him again, and meanwhile the nights were the worst with the chill and those creatures trying too gets inside and Betsy was so frighten that she hid in the closet. Liza said I think that Leo had the right idea about leaving we cannot stay here forever that is true but he took the car and how will we get away? But how do we do it and not being in danger and a safe get away. we need to sneak outside and looked around and find a car and gets inside and then ride way that is the plan, and I hope that Leo would comes back and that ways we have a chance but now it seems too be hopeless. But it is not, believe me, I do but I am scare so am I.

But they were quiet for a while and then Betsy cried out and said I want to go home. I know you do but we need to stay here for right now, we cannot go out there and we might gets caught by those bad peoples and I think that we will be fine here, mom I don't like it here and I wants to go and find grandma, I don't wants to be rude but your grandma can be dead, don't says that mom, I seen her on the street when I snuck out with Leo.

That is my point, Betsy, she will never be with us again, why are you being so means mom? You need to hear the truth, and I am telling you, honey.

Betsy ran out of the room and cried and then Liza follows her and came closed too her and said we will be fine and Joe will take care of us and Betsy I love Leo and now you dump Leo and he was a very nice man and now you have Joe, mom you always have a new man and I don't like this, don't be like this, but I love this man, did you hears what Leo said he is in love with Kate, but she could be dead and I am here,, but mom you never listen too me, and lay on the bed, and seeing shadows through her windows and being very quiet and Joe said we cannot stay here. Tomorrow I will find a car and we will leaves this place but I need to find my mom, she could be just daze and not sick, if she is we will gets her help. But are you sure about that's Liza, I think that is a bad idea, I don't care but I need to fined her and put ours lives in danger, why are you so negative? I am trying not but I think we should find her and that ways and Betsy won't go on her own, I do understand, so now we need to sleep and leave in the morning, because there are less of them. Do you think that they are zombie? I am not sure, but we just have rest and leave this place and we will be safe and I hope that Leo is okay! We should not let him go alone, I know but he didn't wants too be here when we were in the other room and he felt out of place, I know we were wrong and I wish I talked him too stayed.

Now it is too late and we should just focus about our move now!

Day five lights out

On the fifth day, Joe steps out of the house and it was clear and then he looked around for a car and then he saw a van and he said I will go inside the van and drive too Liza and Betsy and we will leave this place and that was his plan, and about a minute later he was surrounded and he was inside the van and meanwhile Liza and Betsy were inside and waiting for Joe too comes and started up the engine and drove toward the house and he honk the horn and Liza said now we need to go to Joe and Betsy said " Looks Mom they are around the van" you are right! Honey! So now what should be doing? Betsy said to run too Van and get inside and then Liza was not happy about that's and said okay! But meanwhile Joe was honked and honked and got more attention and they were coming in pack and now it was getting more dangerous and it was really touch and go! So they came out of the house ran toward the van and they were inches way from the zombie.

When they got inside, Joe drove away very quickly and didn't looked back and they headed out of Long island and Betsy said I think that I saw grandma,. Now she is not grandma anymore. how can you be sure?

I can't but we cannot help her and Betsy said turned the car around and then we will take her too the hospital and no we cannot, you don't love her mom, I do love her and I was unable too help her and I couldn't never let her alone and so now we are alone and we need to remember her, I will mom.

But I see more those zombie. You are right honey and Joe where are you headed, toward Connecticut. Do you think it safe there? I don't know but we are going too Stamford, CT and we are going to stay there! Joe said I am sure that I have enough gas to gets there! What?

Joe said don't gets worry but then they pass the car that they got Leo, no I cannot believe that but they didn't sees any body on the street.

So where is he? I don't know but just keeps on going!

Liza I don't like this but we will be fine, yes we will said Joe.

They drove into Main Street and they stops in front city hall and Joe said maybe we should, so they stepped out the car, they close the car, and they step into the building, and looks around the corner, and step inside the elevator and when to the "mayor office" are sure yes and we need to be quiet.

Now what? We will wait until someone comes to save us, will they comes? I hope so. They sat in the mayor office, and Betsy said I am hungry.

But honey I don't have no foods here but I do have some snack but I want really foods. That day Betsy was such being bad and didn't wants to listens to anyone, so does this place has power, well it has a generator, oh I sees but it will be dark again! You're saying that it will be pitch black and I don't want to sit in dark. Don't think about it but we need to do!

So Joe and Liza and Betsy cuddle each others, then the power went out and Joe took out the flashlight and Betsy relax and fell asleep in her mom arms. The next morning Joe got up and walks around and looks but didn't feel right staying up there and said we need to go, but why I just don't like it. You must have reason and tell me but I believe we are not alone here, are you saying "zombie" are up here. Yes but we need to be very when we walk downstairs and get to the lobby and runs to the car and close the car and I will be in back of you, promise I will be, and I will not gets caught.

They walk very and not too make a sound and Betsy said what going on, honey we must be quiet, and we will be fine.

They reach the bottom of the stairs and walks out and they got into the car, and Joe was walking toward the car, and two zombie would about to grab him. But Joe got pull inside by Liza and then he started up the car.

They drove away and didn't look back but about ten zombies follow them and Joe speed out fast and I don't sees them.

Now Joe was relief they would gone for now, so where are we headed now!

Day six lights out

Joe drove and drove until they ran out of gas. Now they got out the vehicle, and walks on the street, but Liza said to Joe I think that we should gets inside, I think that your right! About a minute later they saw the zombies approaching them and said we don't even have weapon too shoot them and we will end up dead and then Betsy said what mom nothing we will be fine so get inside and we will block the doors and windows and we will be safe tonight and then we will figure out how to gets out of here when the time is right, sure Joe said well I don't like being trap inside and we have no escape plan so we are trap, no I don't think so.

Meanwhile they sat in the dark and Betsy was really getting frighten because she saw someone looking inside and they knew that the zombie wanted to get inside so Liza said this place is not that solid like I thought but now we need to stay put until someone rescue us, no one know that we are here until Leo got the SOS too someone but he doesn't know that we left that place and now we are alone. Joe said we will get out of here and I will find a car and then we will get way and then we can be relaxed.

I do understand but looked how many "zombies" are there! many I know but we will be fine, I think I cannot stop shaking and I sees my daughter, and what she is going on and she know that it is not normal and she is only a child and I don't know how too tells her and I don't even think that I could lose her but I hope not and I pray too god that the zombies will not break in.

But now don't let them hears us and we must be very silent and then we need to get out here and you need too distract them and then I could somehow find a car and then we can escape and what happened if you

48

get caught and we are alone and you know that I don't drive a car and Joe said you will survive this and so will Betsy, so suddenly you being positive and I am just thinking this might be the end! Stop this now!!! I cannot help myself and I just think we might end up get bitten and turned into zombie, and then Betsy said what mom, what did you says, we will be fine, honey don't lies too me mom, those zombies wants to eat our brains and guts and you are not telling the truth and there is no one to help us that is true, Betsy.

Joe said to Betsy I know that you don't know me but you need to trust me and I said that we will not end up being dead meat for the zombies and we will make out of here, I don't believe you, because you hurt my friend Leo and he really loves my mom and he is somewhere and maybe even dead because you took my mom away from him, stops this Betsy and she left the room and said leave me alone, listens Betsy soon we will be going and you need too help me to distract the zombies, I do understand, mom and I don't wants to be here neither, said Betsy. But we need to be quiet and then we can leaves and then we can find other peoples, that are not infection and then we will not be alone and then we can be stronger, but what happened if we are the only ones? Don't says that Betsy? But it can true I know but I don't want to believe that possibility, don't think negative, I won't said Betsy, but then Liza I just want too live and if we are have live with zombies, for sure I don't wants too be there meal, I just wants to killed them. Then Liza said to Joe I hope that the lights comes on and hope that no one is a zombies and only a bad dream, hope that your right but I don't know but I hope the best, so do I and then they saw that Betsy wanted to sneak out and Liza said no, you are not going alone out there and you are going too listens too me once in my life, do you understand? Yes I do.

Betsy sat on the chair and was mad that she was stuck with Joe and her mom and Betsy wanted to search for her grandma and they refuse too gets her and they waited and waited and thought on the eighth day the lights were comes on and then Liza said I will tried my cell phone and maybe I will reach one of my friend, so try it, I will and then Liza did and nothing!

Seventh day of lights out

Now Liza was getting worried and thinking that they could be only one alive and didn't wanted to says anything to Joe and Betsy and then Liza said I we need to walks around outside and maybe we will spotted someone that is not a zombie, well you are willing to risk your life and your child? If we stay inside we will be also trapped and maybe even gets bitten and died, so I am looking for a chance of survive. Joe thought well daylight would be better and at night it is a bit risking and maybe that Betsy were not keeps up the speed and then we can lose her and you are right said Liza, you are concern about my daughter, and I like that very much but we need to leaves Stamford and we need to get closer too New Haven and go to the train station and maybe they are running, you know what you are saying? Yes I do, I believe that the train are not running and so we will need a another transportation to gets around, so we need to find a car and just drive away and reach our destiny and then we will be safe, I think that we will be never be safe, why are you saying do you sees any peoples alive? Well no so far no!

But we need too be very careful went we walking the street on down town and I believe that we will run into those zombies. I hope that you are wrong about that's! I don't think so but we need to very close do you understand what happening here? Yes we are surrounded by zombies and they some how it occurs when the storm came in and they just keeps on growing in numbers and we will not be safe and so we are better off just moving on and do you understand and don't stops for anything, okay I won't! We need to find supplies and survive this epidemic, and we will make it alive, Liza agree with Joe and Betsy was not too happy about being this situation and thought of ways of leaving her mom and Joe and searching for Leo and her grandma but at that time Betsy didn't think that she were be in danger by the zombies and her mom were be terrify that she left them, and were end up being a zombie. So far Betsy was planning to sneak when they both were asleep, that was Betsy plan, at moment thought it was good but it was a bad idea, and were cost her life. That night Betsy was waiting for Liza and Joe too fall asleep and to sneak out and find Leo and her grandma and at that moment thought it was a good idea but she didn't know the conquer that she might be killed and or get the infection and turned into a zombie, but at point Betsy didn't think and about after midnight, Betsy check and saw that they were sleeping and she slowly opened the door and tried not too make a sound and then she snuck out and walks the street and saw a few characters and didn't think nothing about it and then Betsy when to the four corner and she spotted some peoples and was about to called out and then someone grabbed her and it was Joe and he said what the hell are you doing? Well I wanted too find my grandma and Leo, they are not here and you need to go back to the re restaurant and then I will not tells your mom what you did, I don't believe you so, they are watching us and I don't know if it airborne, comes on I cannot do this every times that you take off this time you been lucky and maybe next time you won't be, and then they were silent, then Liza said what going on well your daughter snuck out and almost got caught by those "Zombies" and I rescue her on time, well Betsy you don't listen well so I think that I should ground you but this circumstance I won't because, things are just different. So if thing get back too normal that you will not be allowed to watched TV for a month for right you, will stay with us and no more sneaking out, do you understand? Betsy, yes I do, and she sat at the table and watched the rain falling and then she heard a sound of cat and said too her mom, can I get that cat out of the door and Joe said it might be infection and might bite your daughter and about a minute later,, the cat was gone and Betsy cried.

Eighth day lights out

Betsy said I just wants too go home and I don't wants to stay here, but we cannot go, now we need to stay here, well I don't like it here. Time when by and Joe and Liza were in love and Betsy was very upset and thought about Leo and her grandma and Joe said we can have a serious problem that is she decided to find them on her own and we cannot let her to do that's I know that she will gets killed by the zombies. then Betsy sat back and listens what they were saying and no emotion in the street and it was very quiet and Joe thought it was safe and he was about too step out and they were standing there! Then he pushed Liza on the floor and then Betsy said what are you doing too my mom, don't let them in. who the zombie?

Then they locked the door very tight and then Liza got up and she was bruise and Joe said sorry I have hurt you but I did save your life, sure you did but I am bleeding and Betsy was very upset about the incident and said didn't like Joe, and Liza said we are trapped here and we need too get the hell out of here! You right Joe but think how we will get out here without be caught by them, I don't know but you and Betsy have too get to the car and I will behind you, and don't lies Joe, I won't! I believe that I cannot trust you anymore, but why, because you are thinking of Rachel, yes I am and I should taken her with us, so we could have a threesomes, you must be kidding Liza, she is my wife and I have taken her granted and now I don't know if she is dead or alive. That is true but you had to follow me and Leo and I could have been happy with Leo and he is probably dead, now you are blaming everything on me? I think that I am and then you think of that precious Kate, comes on now, I have saves your lives and now you are just bitten off my head and that is the thanks that I you really appreciate me so much that you ended my marriage and now you blame me for the epidemic, and we are far away from home!

This is the last day that they stay at the Stamford and they thought it was time too move on and found more peoples and but it is a lost cause and Liza didn't wants to hear a lot of negative out of Joe mouth that she cover her ears and Liza walks, Betsy didn't talked too Joe or too her mom ands she knew that Joe was not on the level and didn't know where it was safe.

But then Betsy said "we are going to dies" stops saying that Betsy, and be quiet and don't speak too my daughter this ways! We are just too much stressed and I don't like it and I probably lost my mom too the zombie and now I am feeling guilty about leaving her, don't feel bad and you didn't know this was going to happened and it is not your fault you still have Betsy and you have me,, yes that is true when you find Kate, you will abandon us and we will be gone,, stops this instantly, okay, I will!

"Then Betsy said mom you have left us and when to the party, but don't you remember that you were there too? You are lying and I don't remember what you are saying, I am telling the truth and mom you twist, stop behaving like a brat, you only treated me like you dislike me, because of my mom not now, Betsy! But when, are you going to treat me like a adult and not like a child, well stops trying to run away and stick with us and then went we find a safe place and some chances that I might find Grandma and Leo alive, why are you telling her that's we don't know that we will make it.

Well I try to conform her and make sure that she doesn't go on her own, but she hate me and you for taking her and not searching for grandma, well I was at your party and Betsy came along and then Rachel started the fight and Leo and I left and you follow us and now we are stuck in this mess.

About ten minutes Betsy said went are we going to on the bridge and Liza said, I am not sure because, don't you sees them on the bridge? Yes I do and it is swamped of zombie and now we must turned around and go back, are you crazy? No I just wants be out of here!

Epidemic

Do you think that the epidemic is causing this infection too spread? I don't know what going on but I don't wants to find out, and catch it, I don't neither, said Joe and Rachel and Betsy,, we should move on and no stopping and then we can hears some broadcast. Do you think there any report about what going on and I don't know but why don't you just put on the radio and I don't wants to make any sound in the car and the zombie might hear it, but they do smells us, and we can be dead meat, stop that Betsy, I don't wants to hears that negative talking from your mouth do you hear me? Loud and clear, thanks Mom!

Later that night, Joe walks out of car and left the girls in the car and looked for some water and foods but he didn't tell them too lock the car and then Joe walks for miles and miles and then Liza woke up and said " where did he went" ? I don't know but he didn't even tell us and he probably looking for Kate, stop this said Liza too Betsy. Be silent and I don't want hears a sound and I will start up the car and then I can listen to the radio, mom don't, Joe said it were make them comes toward us and then we would be in danger, for five minutes. No, don't do it mom, you will make them comes to us and we don't have no weapons and they will drag us from the car, no I will protection you,, my sweet daughter, you cannot promise my safety and I don't wants to runs when they comes to get us, well Joe really scare you, be quiet I hears something, they are coming!!!!

But where is he? I don't know, hope that he will comes soon, we are like sitting ducks here, then Liza put on the radio and it make sound and they started to roam and approach them and Betsy said I told so! I think that they spotted us and now we need to drive away and leave Joe, no I am waiting for him, mom you are crazy, you need to go now I don't wants to dies right this moment and I just wants to lives, we will!

Meanwhile Joe search and search for some water and foods and then he ran into a few of zombie and couldn't believe how strong they are and then he hit them over the head and then fell down. Then he somehow he found some water and then he put it into his pack and then he walks slowly and he knew that hew was not alone and he somehow started to runs and runs and then he reach the car and saw the zombie surround the car and then make a sound and they came closer too him and then Liza started up the car and knock down a few and got Joe and they took off and headed to Westport and said it might be much safer, we are not safe anywhere but we just need to keeps on driving and hope to hears the lately news about this epidemic, so many peoples have it and it must go into the brain. I think so, because they are hungry for brains, you are right. Because it effective there brains and it hurt them and then, the zombie think that brain were take the pain away, well Joe how do you know about Zombie, well I used to watched a lot of zombie movies.

Oh, I wander if the CDC is involve they must be and I didn't sees anything but zombie, well I guess they ate the Military, and I think that we are on our own, don't says that's! I don't worry about it; we will be saved, by someone, are you sure? I am not sure but we will be safe, until alls the zombie are killed and they don't roams the street, then we will be safe.

Joe said now, we need to looks out and looks around and they would about to step out but then Joe stops and said go back inside and they alls went back and sat down, we will wait until morning and then we will leave, this terrible place and go back home, are you, crazy their no home to go back.. Are you sure about anything in life, not anymore, nope but I am not giving up on life, to survive and make it alive and not turning into a zombie.

Stop talking, we need to go on and then we can go, now and Joe walks and Liza follows, and Betsy, said so where is the car? Up the street silver car and two doors, go inside the car... I will be a minute their.

Joe walks so slowly, and Lisa and Betsy yelling out, and they are coming and they are coming closer and they will catch you, don't worry I will be fine. Joe walks and walks and they were getting really near and somehow he didn't get caught by and the zombie and then he got inside the car and drove off and said I don't have a clue where it is safe? We should heads back to Manhattan and I think it is more secure and I think that you want to know if Leo makes it? and then Liza said I also wants to know if my mom is fine and then Betsy said that we should left must earlier it could be late, don't says that Betsy, then Betsy said your probably will sees if Rachel, yes she is my wife and we did have a argument and now I need to sees if they are alive, that alls! So you still love her and you used my mom and that is not true and we have problems than this we have to do with the zombie's epidemic, and I don't know, if we will survive this and we need to find someone and maybe they can explains which location is safe, then Liza said well, I cannot let my daughter to get caught by the zombies and we need to stay together and no matter what? Don't explore on your own, do hears me and I am saying especially to Betsy, I won't!

Liza, said to Joe I will not let her go by herself and I will be with her at alls times, and Joe said we are not going to separate in no ways! Do you hear me? Yes loud and clear and no more complaining and no more nothing. We need to make it alive and you know that we don't have weapons but we need to killed the zombies in the head, yes we know but don't get bitten, no ways, I will not gets closer and we find a ways out and we will be fine, why are you saying that's to Betsy.,, we don't know if we will make it tonight, but don't scare my daughter and don't frighten her, and Betsy said Mom I am not a child, and I can takes it, and Then Liza said well let do the search for others and then Joe said yes that we will looks for others survivors.

Searching for other survivors

Joe and Liza and Betsy walk the street of Manhattan, and so far they didn't see anyone on the street and or in the stores.

But then Betsy walks inside and Liza said where is my daughter, I don't know, did she sneak away again? Probably she did, I told her not too and she still does it and she is so stubborn and does not listens too anyone and now you saying that I have raise her wrong? No but she didn't listens anything that we says and she just goes on her own and she put us in jeopardy and she didn't care what happened! She does but sometime she doesn't think and that how she gets in trouble time after time and I will tells her not to lead first and you should looked first and then we will follows, yes I likes that much better and now we need to find person's that are not infection and find some weapons to survive this ordeal. I totally understand and I believe that we will comes out of this situation and we will have no problem, but I am definite sure what will happen too us. It will be good and we will be safe and hope that no harm will happen to us. I am worry about Betsy, because she like too wander off and then she somehow just goes the wrong ways and then we need to rescue her, I know but she is your daughter and make sure that she does not go above the boundaries, but how can I? I don't know and she doesn't like being control and then she feel that she need to runs, no we will not make her runs, no I will stops her and then we will alls be safe. Are you sure? Yes I am definite sure about Betsy and she will not lose control and I will watch her and she will be an angel.

Later that night, Joe walks doors too doors and every place that he looked it is desert and no one in sight and then a minute later, one zombie jump behind him and he called out to Liza and Liza pick up a stick and hit the zombie in the head and it bled out and once again they are safe. Then Betsy screamed out and said they are coming this ways! Mom, Joe! Runs Betsy and come inside and don't let them catch you, that day Betsy ran for her life and didn't looked back and got inside and they shut the door and then they were banged and banged and now what? I don't know but we can hold them long and they will get inside and then Betsy said that is my fault, but why I thought I saw Leo. And I called out too him and then they smell me. But why, because she was still looking for him, and she alert the others zombies to comes this ways and I don't like your daughter too much right now. Did you do something like that you know that we were not safe and then Liza said don't yell at my daughter, well now we have a trouble because of her, no because of the epidemic, and virus spreading.

That is terrible and who fault is it? I don't know but probably the government, and who know but I just don't wants to be one of them, I know what you means but I think we will be fine! We make this far and we didn't catch it so I think that we are immune from the virus, hope that your right! I don't know but I am going to give up and I am going to be alive until it over and I want the same. Later that day, Liza said Joe, talked very quietly and then said don't let Betsy, and I know that she will gets pissed and then she will gets angry and with us that is true.

But then Betsy said this area, I think it safe and I think that we should search for others, you are right but we need to comes back by night and seal the door and make sure no one will gets in, are you sounding paranoid, no but I just don't wants to be trapped and I don't wants to be dead meat.

Fine, I don't that neither but we have no choice but this weird thing happened and now it is a nightmare and I wants to wakes up and have everything too be back too normal, so do I and just want too sees my family during the holiday and I was separate from them because of the "Halloween party that you invite and then Leo came and then he got angry about us and then Rachel got angry and kick us out, that was the worst night ever!!!

Moon Eclipse

Joe and Liza and Betsy, and said well, well it is getting darker than usual, I know what going on, and those zombies are going out of control and I don't know what going on, and then Betsy said looked seems like the moon is getting cover and now it getting pitch black.. and the Zombies are getting more, aggressive and they are going out control, and seems like they wants to break the window and gets inside, no did you put the wood and block the window, yes I did and I don't know if it will hold. I am afraid and I am scare too Joe and I think that this place was a mistake going to Manhattan, and I think that you right about that's and we need to get back to the car and go north and where it is cold and virus that didn't reach.

Are sure, I am not right now but one thing I think that we should to go to Maine and wait until they destroy the zombies, and then we will be able to go home, it might takes months but it is worth it, and you are right said Joe to Liza, so you are totally agreeing with me, yes and then Betsy why don't you asked me, your only seventeen and we are adults, thanks! I when through a lot I know you did and then you saws the zombie took your grandma and then you just saw a lot and you hid when the zombie came in and you went through much mores than we did, that is true and I think that we are doing the right decision about leaving.

But the moon eclipse and it really dark and it is really difficult too sees what we are doing and there are no street lights and hard too sees the cars and we need to do it now. Okay!

Later that night they left Manhattan and went to Maine and Liza and Joe were very sure that they were be safe, and the moon eclipse was so long that seems that night was didn't leaves yet!

They drove and drove and it was darkness and then Joe said it does not seems like it is not changing, seems the same we are still in darkness.

Darkness rolls in and it was pitched black and Joe said seems we are dooms here don't says that's you will scare Betsy and me!

They were about reach the destination and Joe said it is morning and no more darkness and the moon eclipse, is gone, final it is. I think that we are able to step out and walks away fine and then we will head home, well it is really not over but I think it is the beginning, what are you saying? You heard me what I am saying that we will never be safe again! don't scare me or my daughter again do you hears me Joe, if I was not afraid I would have let you long ago but I don't know where too go and where I would be safe with my daughter, can you tell me, that answer? No I cannot but you are not leaving until, it is the right time, but when will it be, no it cannot but we need to go now. I have no answers but

Maybe we have a ways to travels but not seen or smell by the zombie., well we need to killed one and then use his blood and walks out and they will not bother us, that is a plan but I hope it works and I don't wants to stayed here anymore and I just wants to takes a walks and relax in the sun, I agree and I just wants to be home with my family and not in the street of the undead.

Joe said the moon eclipse is over and now we can just walks out but we cannot they are standing out there! We will be trapped!

Mayhem and death
and no end of Zombies

Joe stick out his head and he almost got caught when a zombie tried to grab his head and eat it and Liza said watched out, he almost got you that was a close called, I know and thanks for warning me, anytime I don't wants to be alone. So I will warns you of any signs of them trying to get inside and I will stand by you and you will be my man, but the journey was to find Kate, well once again the princess name came up and you only wanted to have sex with me, because you thought we were have died and so far we are beaten those zombie. That is true but we don't have weapons too destroy them and we don't have the energy to beat them, well now you sound like you are giving up on your life, but I am not said Joe, but I just realized that I cannot go on and on and they multiple by a moment and then there are mores and mores, and I am getting stronger but weak and I don't wants to died this ways, I know said Liza I don't neither but we cannot give up do you understand? Yes I do. But we will be walking out together and no one is not walking out alone, yes we know and we must do it very soon, they will be inside and we will be dooms., you don't have too tell me but we need to runs for your life like that you never did., but I did, don't you remember, yes I do , Joe. Ands they were talking and Betsy snuck out and ran to the car and pull it up to the curb and Liza said looks it is Betsy and she find a car and came for us and us. So how do we passed the zombies., I don't know but we need too, yes we do and Betsy is waiting for us, let go you first said Joe, fine. Liza steps out and watched her steps and make sure that a zombie were not catch her and so Joe followed her and he was not too far and then Joe said Looks at Betsy, her face had change., and he ran up too her and said. I think that Betsy is a zombie? What you crazy?

"Then Liza was about go inside and Betsy tried to grab her, and Joe pulled her out and then Betsy started to says "I wants brains!!!!

No, she is not herself. No, my baby daughter is a zombie, she never listens too me and now I have lost her to this virus, why?

Liza had tears in her in eyes and said I have lost my child because of this epidemic, I am not going to lose my life and I am not going to shoot my daughter, well she is not your daughter anymore., and we need to killed her immediately and I just wants to says bye to her, and it is very risking, I know but I do wants to give her a hug., she will bite you, I will be very careful. I will and I just wants to kissed her and give her a hug, no you cannot do that's! I will. you must be crazy, okay! Liza was about to hugs her but then Joe came up and whack her on the head and then Liza started to yelled and screams at Joe what you done to me? How could you? Well she is zombie, and she is gone. I sees that she is and now I will hold her but I think that we need to burned her now, I need some times and so leave me alone, you will be swamped by the zombies and you will have no ways of escape, and I know the routine and I will be fine. Liza sat next to Betsy and Liza was crying and she didn't sees them coming and she just sat in the middle of the street and Joe notice the activity and Joe called out but she didn't hears him, so he ran too her and pull her from the street and into the dress shop and said why did you pull me away, I didn't finishing to says goodbye to Betsy, well you didn't wanted to be "DEAD MEATS"?

No, but I would have the energy to run but you drag me inside and I have a bruise on my arm, and Joe said I am very sorry, I thought I was saving your life, you were but my daughter is dead, because she went to that party to your home and I lose everyone that I loved, no you have not, you have me! Then she said so how long will I have you went you find Kate, I will be alone, I don't know if she is dead or alive!

But I don't want to talked about her, she was out of my life. Why are you bringing her up, I even left my wife for you, I do have feeling for you and Leo ran off and probably is a zombie, and I am without my daughter and I have loss a lot persons, so have I! they very silent, but out their it killing and mayhem, in the street, and we are in middle the mayhem and alls those zombies, are smelling us and they wants to gets inside and eat our brains.

It won't happen we will are secure and we will not be velour by the zombies, how can you be sure they won't! they are banged on the door and window, I hear a crack and seems like someone will be inside, if they do we need to dash out and run to the car that Betsy got and we will leave this area, but where?

So we will drive and drive and until we gets out of this hell and we will knock down the zombies, but one zombie jump on the back of the car and Joe tried to knock him down, but still the zombie was on the car, now what?

I don't know there are too many and I think, that we have a problem and I think this time that we are trapped and looks we are surrounded, and I don't like it, and I will gets out there, I promise we will make it alive. No I believe you, I am telling you the truth. You cannot promise me anything because we are in block in and no escape, I will back up and then forward and go through them, then Liza closed her eyes and then Liza then Joe went through them but then Joe stops, and Liza why did you stops!

I don't know but I probably play chickens with the zombies, are you losing your mind, Joe? No, just figure out how to gets around them and not gets killed. So what is the plan, I think that I just should drive but they standing so close too the car that scare the hell out of me. I know but we will not become zombies, at that moment just speeding out and knock down dozens of zombies and the blood spatter the windows with blood.

Then drove into the intersection right on the highway on 95 south and heading to Florida, are you should this place will be not infection?

Moon eclipse days of darkness

Infection spread!

Infection spread coast to coast

They drove for days and but a few stops. Do you think that we will be alls right! Yep, I think it didn't reach the coast of Florida and we will run into persons like we are and we will be fine, you sounds so positive but are you insure that we will not gets stomp on us, that true, well we will make sure that we will be okay, and this place is immune from the zombies. We can rest and not worried why are so sure about this epidemic, I am and I think that we will be safe and we will be fine to walks the streets, and have fun.

How can think about having fun when ours family and friends are gone they got infection, and we are alive and not sick so far, and looks like there are no zombies here, I don't sees them, that is good signs.

I hope that your right, yeah! Huh! I don't get it, I just wants stops living and there must be someone around but it is this place is stranded, and no one know around, kind of spooky, what do mean? Hope that no zombie to jump out and bite us, stop saying, ok I will.

Later that night Joe walks out of the hotel and Liza, follows him and said where the heck your going? Well, I just wants to looks around, if we are able to looks in the stores and gets supplies and even find weapons if case to shoot the zombies. yeah I know but I feel better inside go back and I won't be long, no I am afraid, I promise I will not be long. So Liza said I am going back inside lock the door and then peek and that moment that Liza saw something was about unlock the door and was about to yelled out, Joe wouldn't heard her and she was about to run to him but went inside and hid in the corner and waited and waited until Joe come back.

About one hour later, so far Joe didn't comes yet! Now Liza just sat there just wandering where is he? Then it was darker and no sign of Joe.

About ten minutes Joe was walking, and was weak and barely walking and I open the door, and Joe and he fell in the floor and Liza and pick him up.

Joe looks at me and smiled and spoke, and Joe said have I been bitten, and that moment, Liza looks around his body, and there would no marks on his body, but he was drooling from him, and Liza said to Joe what wrong?

I think that I drank the water and suddenly I felt ill and I couldn't walks back, but I was praying all the ways back, but there are no zombies around and we can go places but we need to test the water and need the kit, for our healthy. I know where do I find it and I don't know we need soon because you are coming down with something and I don't wants to catch it do you understand? Yes I do and I think that we better find it and before I become one, I don't think that you will be we need to prepare just in case, are you getting paranoid? No I am not but I am scares, because ever since that I loss Betsy and I don't wants to lose you, got it. so why did drink that water I thought it was good. Well it was not and you have some kind of germs, I will be fine said Joe to Liza, but not really, okay your right!

I still believe that if the climate is warms, you will not catch it that not true I heard that Peoples in LA got it and now they are zombies. I think you could be right but I am not worry right now but I just don't wants to stick around then being trapped and no escape and end up being dead meat and not turning into a zombie and than I believe to looked around and then if you feel safe and you stick around and then stay a while but I think for a moment, that you are missing your precious Kate, why do hate her so much because you never really loved me and I was only a sex partner and that you were using me and I don't like being used.

Stops it! I will but I do wants you too hears me what I am saying and don't stops me when I am speaking and just listens to the "words" I am saying, I do totally and we need to have a plan instead of fighting with each others, so let shake on it and promise not to take an advantage from me, and promise that you won't, I do.

Fighting for your life

Joe and Liza said well everyday is a fight and I think that we will be able to beat it and I think that you might be right and I think that we stick together and I think we will survive this ordeal of the virus and the zombie, there must be someone out there likes the military to killed them. Hope that you are right? I know that I am and I think we won't gets killed but save by someone and worry about the end of the world, and you know that alls started with that October storm end of the month and I know because we had the Halloween one day before and then the storm came in and then peoples started to change and I don't know how to explains it. so we will be leaving Florida and we will go back to Manhattan, and sees if the military came in destroy them, but seems like no one around and I think that we should keeps guard and I will keep watch at night and you can sleep and I will watched the door, well are you sure? Yes you need the sleep so do you and if I hears a sound and I will wake you.

Promise me, that nothing will happened to me and you, I cannot, anything might happened and so I think that we should take one day at a time and hope for the best, and I think that I am in bad dream., you are so am I .

Then Liza when to the sleeping bag and lay down and fell asleep and then Joe doze off and the rain was falling and Joe didn't hears anything and about 2 am, Liza got up and pat his shoulder and he almost slip and fell to the floor and he said what are you doing, you scared to death, well I could have been a zombie and you could been dead and then what were I do?

Now you are once again getting crazy and I will not let you gets hurt and killed I did promise you, you can't because you fell asleep and I could be bitten and turned into zombie and then I could have bite you and eat your brain and you still would been dead, don't you get it, this might never end.

I don't wants to listens to this negative and I do wants to make it back home.

But we need to fight and not give up and we needed to gets weapons and then go out there and shoot them in the head and they will not get up and chew us up, so we just have a kitchen butcher knives and so we don't have a gun and bullets and we just have the car that might run out of gas and then we might even have too walks back too Manhattan, and it like over thousand miles away. And I thought this place were be safe but I don't think the epidemic, so what will it happened to us and what will it be all right? I hope so said Joe. Listens Joe I been on the journey with you and we make this far and I would continue of living and not dying on the ways but I need to be sure that we will not end up dead, so you are saying that now we have no future until we beat the odd of living and so far we have ands now we are going back home when this alls started and I just don't know if that is a good idea but I think that we cannot stay here neither and I think they might comes out of water and the sand and the streets and then we will be get killed and be into tiny pieces and then we will become zombies.

I don't wants to hears that Joe and Liza said let go and maybe we will not died today! No not why the hands of the zombies and who started all this, and Joe said the government and it just spread and spread and no end to it.

I know but no matter what? The world will not be the same has it was before this epidemic, that effective so many peoples that no one is being save but being killed and burn on a bon fire and then they search for the zombies and when they are find they are destroy and burned because they come back to live and so no is safe and we are going back that is suicide and I think that we should stay, no, we need to help others but who is helping us to stay alive? We are know how to cope with the problem and seems like I did have a little infection but I am fine and I will not turn into one, if I do shoot me in the head and I will be dead, well I don't like what you are saying, but do the same too me if it ever happened to me. Just does it fine and they agree!

Is this the end of the world?

Liza and Joe and looked around and around and drove and drove and every place that they when, they saw the undead walking the streets.

This is the ways we will end up and not knowing about it and we will just roams the street and we will only eat meat and about me I just like to eat vegetable and if I turn into a zombie, I will wants to have brains? You got it and we just have too move around and make sure that they don't mistake us for zombies, well we don't walks slow like them, and we can gets shot by who ever is hunting them but, seems like there no one else but us and the zombies, well I guess this is the end of the world, I don't want to hear about okay! Fine but it is true, that we are the only living soles, but that cannot be happened to us, but it is and I don't know what I can tell you! But this seem to a nightmare from day one and then I don't know but I cannot deal this situation about being the only survivors and what we build the world and abolish the zombies and then what? Well I don't know but this the first ever but you can blame the government for this, sure I know they are always testing and they keeps secrets and now we just have to win, but you it is not over until we killed them from coast to coast and then, that is fine!

Time when by and they knew there were be no end of the zombies so Liza and Joe just stay for while and move on and Joe said I will find someone who I know and is not a zombies, hope that your right and we have a big task to handle and then we will make it.

Later that day Liza decided to steps out and looked around but she just unlock the door and walks out free and walks a couples block s and then she was not sure where she was and now Liza was scare and there was no ways of contacting Joe and now it was getting dark and alone and then Joe got up and looked around and the door was wide open and then a few zombies got inside and then Joe whacks a few of them and then when to search for Liza.

But he couldn't find her then he heard her yelling and screaming and then he hurried to rescue her and then Joe said don't do this again! I won't I promise you, good and you don't wants to end up like Betsy, don't reminder me, I won't. but this will not be the end, we should focus about living and have no doubt about ending up dead. No, we are not, going end up like the rest but we will not died we know how to survive, and that all I could says about this situation, I don't want too hears any negative from you, just be quiet, okay I will, and Liza walk out of the room and then she notice that there many of zombies, out there. what we are we going to do and then we will get the hell out here and then we will find the safe haven and not be caught in the end but start a new life., you must be kidding, and then we will have a watched out, yes we do, and then we will be fine, and I like we that we make it from the storm and now we need to survive the zombies and we need to travel by day and not night if we do than we are asking for trouble and I don't wants that's and no I just wants live and breathe the air and drink the water and the ground that we walks, sure but I am not sure that we will be able, because we are surrounded by them and I think that we will be able to escape this chaos that I don't wants to be in again!

I feel the same and I just wants to go home and sit around with my family and have dinner and talked and laughed and be together. That is only a dream that I could sees my mom and my daughter Betsy and I wants to hold her and tell her that I loves her and now she is walking among the dead and the I am with you and I don't know what really happened here, but I hope the nightmare were end, but I cannot tells you stops thinking but I know that you loved them and I did too. But you were not there when I was being abuse by Brad and his brother and now it doesn't matter, that I am still alive but no one that I loves to be close too, I am here said Joe.

When you find your precious you will leave me,, that is not true.

Long ways from home

You will change your mind when you sees Kate and I will be left alone to fight for my life and you will protection her and you will let me died. No I don't wants to hears that from you, stops talking this Liza, but I know it is true, no it is not, I will keeps you safe too and that is my promise and you can take my word. I can, I don't know if I even trust you. But looks your alive and those zombies didn't gets inside and then we are safe for now and so what happened later, I don't know but we are not going to let them get us, do you understand, yes loud and clear and don't make a loud sound they we will hears us, I know and I don't wants to be dead meat for them, and I do need my brain too think, yes that is right! So stick with me and you will make it and I know and I will just wander how long will be last and how long that we will get caught from the zombies.

Stops I don't wants to hear that again and again I just wants to be home, said Liza to Joe and then Joe said there was a close called that I was infection but I was not and now I am back to myself but if I do gets sick and I change into a zombie, just shoot in the head and I will not bite you.

What happened if I get infection and you will killed us, I guess who hunting zombies, well it will be a stranger and you will not know that you dead and you will not come back to live and that alls, listens I don't wants to hear this again, I just wants to go back to my place and get my clothes and supplies and leave the city and go toward Maine.

Then the mist came and more things started to happened and Liza said what going on here? I don't know but the zombies are coming this ways and then Joe said you put on the music and they hear us and what have you

73

done? Well I was bore and I wanted to dances, right now? Yes and hold me tight, sure! This could be the last dance that we did, well I am not going to died, so make love too me, yes! I will and I will not let you go!

Let make love and don't let the zombie gets you

Promise me that you will not let me go! Yes and I will hold you, even that they break in and I will hold you and we will died together and I will not let you down, this a little extreme, no but I want to be inside of you and I don't want anything to happened to you, and I feel the same about you, sure, yes I do. I need to asked who are you making love too me? Is it Kate, and Joe got up and said, you just spoil it and I just wants to be nears you, I am sorry Joe but I won't says anything stupid like this, but at that time Joe refuse too comes back and then Liza came close to Joe and convince him that she were not spoil it about talking about Kate and then he was on top of her and then Joe said don't leave me, and then Liza I won't you are my soul mate, and he kissed her and went in and out and then lay on the side of her and hold her in his arms and said, " I Love you" I really do and however thing turn out I will be there for you.

Promise with my heart and soul and I wants you in my life so do I and I just want too says that I just wants to be with you always! I will remember that went we just meet up with "Kate" please don't mention her and if we do runs into her how will explains that her brother is gone and then Liza said maybe Kate is too, don't says that's ! okay I will be your friend and I will not says anything bad about Kate if she is a zombie or not but we are not and if we stick together and we will be fine, that is true and we need to move around and be safe and not gets shot by anyone that think that we are zombies, by accidental, sure I know because there are a lot happy trigger out there would shoot first and then asked, well I just wants to make love with you now and stop talking, yes I will and kiss her lips and then they make love that night and seems that they were fine and then they heard a bang at the window and it crack and then Liza said, they are inside, no it is not happening too us, yes it is and I don't know if cannot stops them.

Joe got up and then Liza hurried up and got dress and Joe said now it is time for us to run and run very fast and go to the car and drive away, I don't want end up like "Betsy" and I don't neither but we have no choice and then we need to do it now, do you understand? Yes loud and clear and don't let them hears you, I won't said Liza to Joe. Joe said there is a car park on the left of this street and tried to get inside and drive up too me, I will tried said Liza, and don't panic and don't be nervous and shaking but you need to be brave whatever happened, I don't wants to lose you Joe, you won't and Liza looked and said Joe they are behind you and they will catch you, don't worry about it and I will be fine, and she kept running to the car and somehow she didn't know where Joe is. Then she approach to the car and saw two little girls has zombies that was about to put there teeth toward her arm, and she hit them with a her hand and got inside and then started up the car and turn the car around and went toward Joe and Joe got in ands said it was a close called and Liza said what happened I almost got caught and bitten by the zombie, did you I don't know but don't stop just keeps on driving and we will check it I did went we are safe, fine.

Meanwhile Liza was watching how Joe was acting and then suddenly she stops the car and said I cannot go on until I know that you are not infection and I hope that you understand? Sure I do, I would do the same I thought you were, well I am being paranoid. No you are being smart, thanks! But we will find a new home and then we will be happy and I think she told me that her name was Kate, I think that she lies to me and I think her name was Kelly and she didn't wants to know who she really was and why is so important too you right now I don't know but I think she was just a liar, well we need to deal some kind of other shit than a liar, well now we need to survive this epidemic, then we can find some more persons are not zombies and I hope that your family is safe and don't you sees the mist?

Mist

"Looks at the mist and you cannot sees in front of you and we need to stay a while until the mist is clear, that is right! I never seen the fog so thick and I don't wants to find out what in it? I don't dare to go out there and whatever bought the this mist and I think we are better off inside and I don't sees no sight of the zombies that is more terrify and I think they will not break in, I hope that Liza said I thought you knew her well but it was bunch of lies that was gives to by her and her family too steal her money, well the whole relationship was a lies from day one and but I did sees her brother in a coma and then that night we make love and then she broke it off with me and ever since than, I didn't sees her again! nope she is history and then this happen and then I came back to Manhattan and then she follow me and then I married Rachel and then we were planning to have a child and then somehow you and Leo shown up with Betsy and then it Halloween party and then the light when out and then it was this epidemic and so now we are on the road and tell this story make it a long story into short stories, that we being chase by the zombie and now the mist bought something in this place and I don't know if it make the zombie more powerful and I think we probably make it alive one more day, I hope and I don't want to dies, I don't neither but we need not too be heard and they will crash inside and we will be dead meat, no thanks! I just wants to live and I will fight for my life and yours. You will not leave me and I will not be able to fight, no I am going be with you to the last days of our lives, I promise this too you, I know that you don't lies and I do trust you and what are we going to do the night that the mist that goes by and might comes inside, and we don't know how to do deal with this situation, I know, but I think that we will be fine, sure I know I have you and we will make it together, yes, just keeps on think this ways and we will be fine, good.

But meanwhile Liza said thought to herself and said I hope that Joe is right and I will be fine and I will make this journey and I will not died hands of the zombie, and Liza thought and cried but Joe didn't sees her and she hide her face and then Joe came close to her and said are you crying? No I am not, then he smiled at her and came up to her and grab her and then kissed her lips and said let make love and I wants to be close too you now, and always, I knew that you care for me for the first time that we met at the strip club and I was a little stone and I was a little wild with my tattoo , near my breast and a little on my ankle and I think that so awesome said Joe, you are much a turn on and I really like that's very much!

Liza looks at Joe said it is coming and it is coming and it will gets inside and it going grab and eat our brains and we will dies, but why and I don't understand and I don't want to die and I don't take my last breathe, hold me and I will and we will survive and I will protection and I will not let you go and I promise, you can, I will, I will not let them get you and about Joe, I will fight to save you, I will not let alone, I don't want to live if you died. Don't say that's I don't, if your gone so will I .

The mist came inside and was getting closer and closer and but they didn't feel what was doing and then Joe said don't let them smell you and be still and then tried to move the other side that they have been, no is it working I feel they are very near and I think they will get us, don't says that's, I won't, and then Joe said did you touch me, and Liza said no, I think something happen too me. What is it I feel numb feeling and I think that I got bite, no, you cannot be.

I am not feeling, don't stay near me I could be infection and then I will wants your brain, no don't says that Joe, then she saw his face was changing and you are infection but they are still here in the room don't let them sees you. I won't!

The mist still inside and Liza said where is it? I don't know but don't stand by me,, I need to hold you and I believe it will be okay! No, I don't want to be alone, if you stand by me I will bite you and you will became a zombie, and whatever that I will become, well I don't like this and then the wind came in and the mist went out and said somehow the lights came on and Liza check out Joe said , No you have not been bitten but you will be fine.

About one hour later they heard a boom and then once again they were inside and now they were surrounded and then Joe and Liza and now it is the end I hope not and then Joe said don't let them get you, hope me tight.

I am don't make a sound and tried not to breathe and I am trying Joe but they are very near and I don't know if I am able to be silent, huh! I don't understand, they are very, very near and then one of them pull out and took Joe and said Liza said don't and then she was grabbed and then, they were pull into the mist and they were slaughter in the street and torn into pieces into pieces and they were not alive anymore and then the mist was gone. Later that night Joe and Liza, were lying on the street and there guts were being pull out of there bodies, and then the mist and the sun came up and it was a new day and it was the end of Liza and Joe and no one knew what happened that day, but the zombies still roaming the street of Manhattan and then, they still near city hall and they were about to enter and then there were gun firing and then every it was silent, but zombies were the one alive and the living became the dead, and there was no end but the world zombies had comes to walks the earth, and living were slaughter like they don't nonsense, and dead walks among us and the mist just, was gone and the day of destruction was the end, and no one came to save the persons still hiding in there home, but zombies had brains and brains, that continue and didn't end with Liza ands Joe but there were more victims that days. But some hide like and makes sure that we would not be seen.

Moon eclipse days of darkness

Night of dead!

Night of dead

J ack and Jamie and were heading to New York and they heard the "
special report and Jack said it can be happening and Jamie said well a
lot persons are missing and I don't know but I wants to find my friend
Joe and his wife Rachel and I wants to stays with my friend and probably
you will be with me, I don't wants to be alone in the city, but looks at those
persons walking and they something out of there mouth, what is it? I don't
know but I don't like this, went we left New Hampshire

But New Hampshire and the breathe air and then this a pollution
city and I don't know I have not heard about the epidemic until we arrive
into this city so maybe we should go back and I don't wants to get trapped
inside the city that I don't know well, huh I thought you travels here
before but with my parents and oh why didn't you tell me this before well
I thought you were not comes with me, you are right, I would not and then
they once again heard that Vermont and New Hampshire and Maine and
Ct and New York, the report said that persons acting strangely and they
are bitten persons and the infection is are getting sick and everyone need
to watched out where gets closed not to get bitten, oh this is really serious
shit and now what? I don't know but I don't like this and I think that we
should find Rachel and Joe place and I think we should be inside and not in
the open and I think your right and I am sorry that I bought you here.

I would have comes because I just didn't wanted to stay at home and
I did have a dreams of my own and getting something in broadcasting
but I guess it is wring timing and I guess we will be safe, I have you Jack
and I have you Jamie, you do and what street does your friend lives well
two street down and okay and then we will park in front of there place I
hope so and maybe they have a garage and that were be nice but maybe

those infection person might be there, oh your right so we are better park in outside and yes!

They steps out of the car and they walks toward the door and no one around and Jamie said well so far so good, yep and I think that we are safe, do you think, are you humor me? No but it is very quiet and I know and I don't like and then they reach the top floor and they steps out and the door was wide open and Jamie said I don't like this,, I don't neither and I will check it out and I am not going stand out here alone, so comes along and watched your back, I will, so you too, and then suddenly Rachel came out from the closet and said,, thanks god that you came, they ate alls my guests and somehow I escape and I hid in the closet for days and days, but she was a bit shaking and not speaking clears, and Jack said I don't understand what you are saying, and Jamie said she is one of them, no, then she started to says I wants are hungry for brains, and Jack steps back and said go back to the elevator and gets inside and I don't if I am able to hold her, well you better get bite, I won't and then Rachel said you are saying that I am zombie, no ways, and then she looked in the mirror and then she saw herself and then she just went toward the window and jump down and Jack said, looked my friend is dead and she didn't wants to eat our brains and I think that we can stay here for awhile you must be kidding, no I am not.

Where can we go, we will not be safe and you think they will not come up here? I don't know but for the night, okay but we need to lock it tight, yes we will and we will not let anyone come inside here.

Promise, that you will watched out for us and don't to be come the living dead I won't! we will stay tonight and then we will leave tomorrow and then we will drive back too New Hampshire and then we can sees if our family is safe, why don't you called them, your are right I will!

So Jamie tried to make a called but no signal and now what? I don't know but you will get connect, how do you know that I will. I am just thinking positive and what wrong with that's!

In the dark

Jamie and Jack just sat in the dark and they thought how alls this began and how they got in the city that never sleeps and now know one is around and they are stranded and trapped in a beautiful penthouse of Manhattan.

We are surrounded by the dead and I thought I were be in a film or in a movie but I am in nightmare and I don't understand what going on here and I just wants to go home and I don't want them to attack us and maybe even venous us and even gets caught scare the shit out of me and I don't wants to be frighten but I am and I don't like it at alls and I just wants to leave and but also afraid to out and I don't wants to steps out but we must and I think that we should just out and go to the car and drive away and then we can go back home, you think so, yes and I think that we should go now but it is really dark and we will need a flashlight and run for our life and that is no problem and I am with you, Jack and don't leave to defense for myself and I don't wants to croak in the middle of the street and I just want to go, I agree but I believe that we should go in the morning in the daylight.

But then Jack step out of the penthouse and then walks around the hallway and then Jamie sat in the couch and tried her cell and but no signal and it didn't work at alls and then she when to the phone and no dial tone and now Jamie was getting mad and furious that she thought why did I when with Jack and I should have stay home and protection my family what am I such a jerk and then Jack came back and said we need to locked the door with some wood and I need to find some nail and I will break the coffee table and banged it on the door and then we will be safe, and then Jamie got closed to Jack and didn't want to let him go!

Later that night they were heard moaning and sounds outside the door and I think they somehow got up here and now we don't have a away to escape and I think that we will died her, and he slapped her face and how could you?

Well you were acting crazy and I didn't wants more attention and so that why I slapped you, and Jamie walks away from Jack and said I won't forget that you hurt me but I didn't meant too and I hope that you will forgive me, no I will not because you are so abusing and you think that we will not make it out and then he hold her said " I love you" boy! You sure didn't act like it for a moment, when you hit me, I apology.

Don't you never do this again, I promise I won't and I will forgive you, and I do love you too, but we need to focus on the zombies out there, yes I know and I never knew that what really happened, well someone just messed up and it could be the government, and it is an epidemic, I think it is virus but some persons got it and some are not even effective and I don't think it is not airborne, then Jamie started to cough and now Jack kind of move away and then said are you catching a cold and Jamie said no I am fine but I do get nerve a little when things that happened and I just feel like panic and I don't like being in this situation and then well your all right? Yes I am and about you and are you afraid that I might turn into a zombie, you must be kidding and you have not been bitten and you were inside and I protection and the answer is no, in my case I almost got bitten and then I escape from Rachel, and I am fine too and don't worry we will make it alive and the dark will be gone and the sun will comes out and we will walks out of the building and we will get into the car and drive back home, that sounds wonderful and just keep on thinking that way and we will make it home and I promise, and said Jack to Jamie .

Then Jamie kissed Jack and said hold me and don't let me go and he said never and said you know that you can trust me and I will keeps you safe and no one will gets in, never and I do believe you and I will listens to what you says and I will not go on my own unless you tells to do so.

Yes, when I says run into the elevator, you go inside and push the button down and don't let back and I will be there!

But it is still dark and we can take the chance, yes but looked before you steps out and then runs inside, yes I will and you do the same, yes!

Just hold and don't let me go and I won't and Joe and Jamie stick together and then they got to the bottom floor and then Jack said go toward the car and in hurried and don't walks slow, I am not but I don't sees the car.

It is right in front of you and the zombies are blocking it and just don't hesitates and just move quickly, and then she got into the car and then they were fine and she started up the car and few zombies were around the car and now what? Just go right through them, fine I will.

Yes but I did have a bit situation and I don't know if we left about one minute later we would been gone, you means goner yes, and I am not kidding and I think that we should leave now and not a word, that's!

Then they sped out into the street and they were walking and walking toward them and they were a bit quick then usually and Jack said did you notice in front of you? Yes and they looks very viscous and I think that they wants us and I am getting us the hell out of here!

But hurried they are gain up on us and I don't like it and I think that they wants our brains and our bodies too and I think that you are right, Jamie and I don't like it not a bit and you make me comes with you and I don't how my family is now, because I thought that we would be working and not running away from zombies, I had no idea about this and I would never you be in danger and I will protection you and I do keeps my word, just get me home to my family, and I hope it is not too late, for them.

I believe that they are fine and I think that the epidemic didn't reach new hemisphere, so how many miles do we travel to get back home couple miles and miles to reach ours destination and we will be there about three hours.

Three hours, to get home

Jamie got really close to Jack and said, so how many miles to get home, about twenty miles and half and I think I don't sees those aggressive zombies around here and I think that we will be fine went we get home, thank goodness and I cannot wait to sees my mom and dad and my two young sisters,, but I hope that they are all right! But Jack you are scaring me, but why, you need to face it no matter what we comes too, and your family and mine, we need to be very careful, they can be infection and I don't wants to get the disease, well what is it,, the virus that make good peoples turn into bad peoples? Not sure, but I am just warning what we might sees when we get back in New Hampshire, you are staying very close too me and do you understand what I am saying Jamie, sure I do and I don't like how you are treating me like a child and I am the same age like you. Stop behaving like this and I can handle anything do you understand and don't be so sarcasm, I am and why are accusing me that I am I don't understand what you are saying but I do care for you and whatever happened, we will make it, sure we will we will end up being dead meat, you are many negative, and no I am not and we will be home and we will not ague about anything and you will be with your family and I will be with mine, and you are so sure about what will be, but we have not heard any bullet report well I think that we are fine, hope that your right and now we are entering New Hampshire and we will be home about ten minutes and you can complains to your folks about the worst trip that you ever took with me< Jamie, and I am not going to tell them that I will be calm and relax and not angry, that is all in your mine, thanks a lot and I got you through the zombie and now you are acting like bitch, thanks a lot for the names calling Jack,, and so we will be on your street about five minutes.

Then they stop and Jamie got out of the car and started to called out mom and dad, where are you? And calling out to her brother John and said they are not here! What do you means? Seem like they left in a hurried and they didn't take there clothes and then Jack said stay close too me and she said why? I think that they didn't leave on there own but someone took them, now you are scaring me, Jack,, I wants to says that they were taken by the zombies, and about two minute later about ten zombies were in her back yard and Jamie said "Looks they are here" what zombies, no I cannot believe this shit, and we have leave immediately and we cannot stay here, I need to find my folks, but they are probably dead, don't says that Jack, you need to realize that something strange happen and we have no control of it and so we need to go and get back inside the car and drive away now, I am staying if you do it is like suicide, I am not going to killed myself but I just wants to be near with my family even though that they are dead, no I am not and I will find them and help them out and do you understand what I am saying Jack, ? yes I do but I think we should go now before hundred and hundred comes here and we died. No you go without me, no we both are going and he said listen we will looks for them and we will find them if they are alive, sure and you can trust me, I do Jack so comes on and we are leaving now, I just want to take some items from my room and some clothes and leave a note to my folks but hurried, you know that we are in danger? Yes I do and it will not take too long and I will be right down, fine I will be in the car waiting for you, okay! Give me five minute and not longer, yes I do know, I will be right there, good and then Jack when inside the car and locked the door and then Jamie was looking around her room and she spotted blood on the floor and then she saw a body moving toward her and then Jamie, ran out and then almost fell down the stair and then when to the car and said you are right let go now and I don't want to comes back here again!

"Night of the Storm"

Jack and Jamie were leaving New Hampshire and Jamie said the rain was pouring hard and Jack almost hit a tree and then there were zombies blocking the road and then Jack said we are almost out of gas. What are we going to do now, find a gas station, and fill up the tank and then we can ride to Vermont and then we can go to my friend, Lee and then we can stay there for a while, about the virus, well I don't know.

Will Lee let us in and I don't know but I am willing tried and not to asked but I think we should visit my friend and then maybe can stay with him awhile and then maybe he know what going on out there! driving in the storm and then we should stops at the hotel and then we can rest there and maybe there will be no zombies and then we can panic and I am not afraid but I think that we shouldn't be in the storm and I think that we should be in shelter, you are right and I agree and then the next the morning then we can head to my friend place and then maybe he has weapons and then maybe we can stay for awhile when this epidemic end, and then what? We start over with our lives and then everything will be back to normal, I don't think so, so many peoples dead in the street and the infection grows and then we might it anyway and I don't wants to hears that nonsense and I just want to be safe and not in danger and then we need to fight to for ours life. That is true and now we need to stop in the middle of the road and not go on until we can sees where we are going, yes and I agree and we might run into a tree and not a zombies, so we will park here and continue in the morning and then we will go to Vermont and then we will be safe, I hope, yes, I think that your right! Then Jack kiss Jamie and said I wanted to this a long time and I know so did I. then he kissed her again and said I wants to make love too you! But not now, but when we don't have this epidemic, and then we can have a family and be happy and now we can be doom and dead the next day and I don't wants end up being a zombies. you won't be, how can you says that I just feel that we bet the odd and we will do it again and the zombies will not catch us and we be fine, how can you says that over and over again and we don't know if we will be alive tomorrow, I don't need your negative, and I don't like the vibe that you giving me, yes and stop it.

I will when you get me out here and I will be angel and I won't be a pain in the ass and do you know what I am saying Jack, yes you will not be a bitch and I won't be a bastard and you gets out of here and I will be very happy.

I just want so reach my friend in Vermont and then we will be safe, not sure but I will let think that ways, you are being so mean too me, no I am not but I am trying to make you understand what we are in what kind of situation of taking killed by the zombies, that is true but I am not going to get killed you are so sure of yourself. Yes I am, well sees reality in front of you and what do you sees "zombies" that is true but this is not the end, but it will get better, how do you know, I don't but I just want the best…

So how far are we from Lee, about ten minutes but maybe more I really don't sees the road and I need to go slow and the road is slippery and I don't wants us to end up in the ditch so I am going slowly but I think I sees them who? Silly the zombies, well I think your right but we will make it Lee and then we will be kind of safe, well I hope that we will be, I am glad to hears that's and Jamie just kept quiet and then Jack we will be at his house about a minute or two and seems quiet and no lights in the house and I don't if that is a good sign or not, at this point I don't know.

Then they drove up to the door and saw the door was open and how what? Do I go inside and check or we just keeps on driving too many questions that you are asking? I know but I am scare at this moment, so am I .

Then Jack stop the car and steps out and Jamie said what are you doing, well I will peek inside and sees how your friend, wait for me, okay!

Meteor Shower

Jamie steps out and said looked at the sky and looks at the meteor shower and they are so many and I don't know what going on and then the zombies started to comes out and Jamie was in back of Jack and said I think that we should get back to the car and I think you right and then Jamie looks and said it is too late for Lee, but why he is one of them, oh I sees so hurried get inside the car and locked and then Jack got into the car and one of the zombies got inside the car and Jack somehow remove the arm and was safe and this moment Jamie was relief and I just want get the hell out of here now, I don't know how we will gets, because the gas tank a little empty, what? Are you saying we are out of gas? Yes! But how miles will get about end of the road., why you didn't tell me I thought we were staying here and we were be fine, now we will not make it. you are saying that we will be walking and I don't have the strength and I think that we should go back the cabin and then we can stay overnight, then we will less gas to get out of here, well we will be in the woods and being surrounded by zombies, and looked more meteor and what going on and then a big one drop on the house and then it was flatted out and then now what one more is coming, drive quickly, I am but it is not good and it is very close and then he drove into the ditch and now we are stuck, don't says anything and I didn't wants to get hit, we won't! promise that we will not get killed, I cannot! Well you are being honest with me, but I don't like it not at alls, I don't neither.

Then they both steps out of the car and walks through the woods and then Jamie, stops and said I cannot walks anymore and Jack said you must they are not too far behind us, no yes they will catch you and then me, comes on, I don't wants to lose you, hurried, they are catching up too us and runs and runs, said Jack, I am but then she fell into a hole.

Jack looked for some a rope and then he just give her his hand and pull her up and said, don't do that again? I didn't do it but I just didn't sees the hole, but they are too close and I we need to find shelter now and I know but you need to carry me. I cannot walks I think that I sprain my ankle and well I will need to find a stick and then you use it and we will be able to walks and I will not walks fast but fast enough to be far from the zombies.

I know Jack, I was the one that we should have comes here and now it is a disaster, well I like traveling you and but understand in different circumstance, me too, and we will be fine. Yes, but let go and less chatting and moving were be better, I do but I am in pain but do you wants to get devour, by zombies, no but hurried, I am they are so close, I hear, them making, moaning, and grunt sound, one just popped out, and tried to grab her and Jack just grab her on time and wow that was close call and I was think I was a goner, but I am not. You save me and you killed the zombies, and we are save, keeps on walking and Jack and at that moment and suddenly jump on Jack , and Jamie ran up and knock the zombie off Jack, are you all right! Yes, did you get bitten, I don't think so.

Jamie looks at him and said well you are lucky this time, yep!

So he got up and they both walks away and they saw a house and then it seem like there is no zombies around and we will walk to the house, then stop and I will check out and I am not staying out here alone, yes you are. I am coming with you and I will not take no from you. Well you are stubborn, no I am, why are you saying, I will not left out alone and I am going with you.

Stop, don't you listens what you doing but we are wasting time and I would have gone in and now, and now you chatting away and you know that you are distract me, now you are blaming me, how could you? Now with gibbering and your screwing my mind, talking and talking, you are making me crazy.

I don't need to hassle me went I just wants sees what inside and babbly away, stop, fine. I will be quiet, so he went inside and Jamie stood outside and waiting for Jack, meanwhile Jamie saw them coming, then she went inside and looked around, and Jack was on the floor and Jamie said what happening? I don't know I felt a little lighting headed and I just fell and then you were talking to me and I heard your voice and I awake and you were giving your hand to me, and I was up and then Jamie notice a bruise and when did you gets this? What do you mean? I don't know what you are talking about. And don't tell me that I am infection with the virus, no I will not says a word, good because I don't feel it and I think I am just exhaust of this whole thing going on this world and it is getting to me, well your not the only is dealing with this so I am, I know Jamie, but let them get inside and I am trying my harder not too, I do understand and I just want to get the hell out of here and we are stuck in this place with thousand of zombies are so hungry that they wants to eat our brains, you don't have reminder me about that's just drag me out to the car and get inside and start it up and drive it, you know I cannot but you must I am injure and I don't wants to died here, well I am worry that I might gets spell of vertigo, but you won't you need to be brave and not to think about it, I will please I am begged you to get us out of here and I am trying but not hard enough, yes I am don't be scare I am next you, and you will do fine, just believe yourself and we will survive this, I am taking your word, and I do believe that we won't died tonight because you drove without fear, and went I start feeling better I will take the wheel from you but they are getting closer to us I know just try to drive faster, and faster, I am , they are catching up too us I know but I need to stop, what going on I am getting the symptom and I don't like it, but don't stop, whatever you do, don't stop! Okay I won't but I am not focus and I feel it will happen.

Moon Eclipse, days of darkness

Waking the dead

Coming out of the graves

Somehow with Jamie vertigo drove right into the cemetery and then stop at the grave stone and the car were not start up and now Jack said what have you done? Now for sure we will be dead, looks how many are coming out of the graves and we need to get out of the car and I don't know how I will make it, but I was wrong to let you drive, well now you are sorry that you did? Yes I am, I don't want to be dead meat. But you begged me to drive and now you are angry, no but we will be dead and I am not strong and I have a bruise and I am not that great and they are smelling us and they will be following us, well it alls my fault, thanks a lot and then Jack said can you at least help me fine I will and looks we are trapped. So you cannot leave so you need to carry me out, you must be kidding, no I am not I am totally serious and I think that you should do it now, or we both will died here. Fine and then she grab his hand and then pull him across the cemetery and then said so far so good, and then Jack got up but took a stick and hold on when he was walking and Jamie was looking around if it was clear and now they were deeper in the cemetery and then Jamie said let go inside this house, you mean the house of the dead and I don't like this and there are bodies of the dead, and hope that zombies are not inside and I am sure about that, but we are in a bad situation each moment and I think that we will be fine, so I will not saying anything else I just need to rest awhile and then I will help you to shut the door, tight and then Jamie said how will we get out of here, good question I don't have answer at this moment but we need to be safe. Yes I know but if we are stuck here and we will dies, no I will have a pried open that we will be able to escape, and Jack was not really telling her the truth and he knew that if is shut tight the air that they have will be gone and the scenario is not good for Jack and Jamie was very dangerous at this time and but Jack kept it too himself and Jamie fell asleep in his arms.

The next morning, Jack got up and heard them trying to get inside and now Jack shut it tight and then Jamie saw that what have you done? Well I had no choice so I locked it, no I cannot believe what you have done and I thought we were going to leave this place and I will figure out how to gets out, I am afraid, but be I am here, and we will have oxygen and we will croak and no one will find us. We will be dead and we will become zombies, probably, stop talking and think of out maybe we can dig out of here. You think that will work, I will pray to god and I hope that we get out of here and not died, we will not, will you promise that we will make it alive, I will find way out. Then she sat down near the corner of coffins and then they heard a movement and then Jamie said to Jack do you hear that and then they heard a creak, sound and comes out two dead zombies, and Jamie screams out and Jack hit him with stone on the head and blood dripping out of the brain of zombies. Jamie stood still and somehow the door open up and Jack, you said that we would gets out and ran out toward the car and started up the back up and Jack step inside and drove away and now Jamie was not afraid anymore and Jack was surprise that Jamie recover her fear of driving, Jack , I am glad that we are leaving this awful , they are not going back , and then she stop and Jack got into the driver seat, and Jamie was once a passenger, and drove mile and miles. Then suddenly, the car stop and out of gas, what are we going to do? I don't know but we better runs, I am they are not too far from us but hurried and Jamie and Jack I am not too far and we should be there at the house soon, yep! About half hour later got into the house and didn't notice the sign of the it said " west funeral home, and they end up the parlor and the interior was red curtains and velvet chair and cherry coffee table, and it is a beautiful house and then they saw a coffin in the other, so we are in a funeral home with corpses, and they can comes alive. Maybe we are safe, I hope that your right!

Zombie girl

Then Jack spotted a girl standing in the hall and Jack said can I help you and she grunt and Jack said what wrong with this girl? Looks she is a zombie, huh! She is coming closer to you closer and what should I don't know, she is only a zombie girl , and her family might be around so we are not alone in this house. Are we not alone? I think so but don't let her bite her, I won't and zombie girl walks toward Jack grab his hand and she was about bite him but then he pulled away and then he ran to Jamie, but the little zombie girl wanted to go outside so Jamie opened the door and she steps out and her family was standing out, and waiting out to them and then they saw us and I shut the door and then they came to the door and tried to break the door and zombie try to squeeze in and then the rest and Jack and Jamie couldn't hold them back, then they place a chair, we need to go out the back door and yes we have no choice they are smelling us and they wants our brains, I think that your right! Now I am feeling a scare and a panic and I don't want to be killed by a "zombie girl" so they dash to the back door and there about ten zombies and about to grab me but they got Jack and then I got a stick and banged the zombie in the head and the blood was dripping out of the zombie head and more zombies would coming, and the zombie girl make the sound like calling mores of them now they surrounded us and at that moment we would trapped. Jack somehow went beneath the zombies did a limbo move and then Jamie did the same but caught by the zombie girl, she smile and grunt about to bite her, and then she twisted her arm and escape from the zombie girl, ran into Jack arms and they ran into the wood and ended up at the dirt road and where would this road lead? I don't know but just keep on moving but I still sees that zombie girl and she is really fast and she will gets us don't be ridicule, that a zombie has so much power.

I guess she does but don't let her gets us.

They would still following us and you mean the zombie girl and now she bringing more other zombies, I don't like this situation, I don't like it neither, they very close and we are going be dead by the sunset and no one will save us, I don't want to lose hope but I think it going to happened. I don't hear about that we are going dies. No, we are not and we will beat the odd but there so many zombies and it is not only the zombie girl, I know .

Comes on we are be trapped and no way out and no place to hide, you are asking too many questions and I don't any answers right but we need to survive, yes I know what we are dealing with this but I know that we will make it and don't you hear me? Yes I do hear loud and clear and we just got move on and on, I am and I am not killed by no zombie, you are right! Then Jack slips on the rock but somehow Jamie pick him up and he was fine but someway needed to visit the ER, and now crutches because you really can walks, but look there is that zombie girl, like inches away from us no kidding, now what? Runs, about you I will be running, but I need some help no I cannot leave you alone and I am going not let died in the wood, and eaten up and torn out and guts and bodies parts. That won't happened how do you know, I will run but you are injure and you cannot even walk and then Jack got caught and then Jamie got to him and drag him into the wood and I will slow you down no you are not, I will hold you and we will be fine, no we are not, stop this, okay I will soon we will be on the main road, but we still runs into the zombies, don't worry about it. few steps out and we will be safe and now we need to find a car and then we can drive away and then, I would like that it sound like a good dreams, but it could become reality and that you can that is right and I don't know but I hope that you are right that we will not be dead meat to t he zombies family and the zombie girl and I think that they when the others direction and I hope that you are right! I am said Jack, and Jamie smiled at him.

Jack and Jamie last journey

Jack and Jamie didn't know the journey would be there but they kept moving and but they ended up in state of Vermont and Jamie said I thought we left the border of new Hampshire and we need to cross the border and walks and walks near a red barn and think there will be eggs inside, I am really hungry so am I want some foods in my stomach, well I wants but I am starving so am I . well so let peek inside the barn they didn't sees anything and it was clear and Jack walk around the barn and then there was one zombie and bald and a mustache and half body torn the inside and seeing the gut and sticky stuff coming out his body and then at that moment and then Jamie find a gun and shot the zombie in the head and it fell to the ground. Jamie ran to him and said we are surrounded by the zombies are here and why did we go there and I don't know but I did grab some eggs and we will go inside the house and make scrambling eggs and bacon, that sound good. Yes it does but we need to go through the zombies and gets inside the house and take the gun and give too me, okay! So Jamie threw the gun and it fell down and fire the shot, almost hit Jamie got hit in the arm and it just went through but it was not a serious but it bleed and then the zombies smell the fresh blood and they were coming toward Jamie and Jack got up and pull her away, then she gave him a kiss and hugs, and Jack hold her and said I will not let you, I won't. about a minute later they manage inside the house and lock the gun and said I need to go out again. no, stay with me I don't want you too leaves me but I won't be long, but promise don't be long but don't take too long and I will be right, yes I will.

When he went out Jamie locked the door and cried that had tears in her eyes and I don't want to be alone, and she got up and called out, Jack outlook they are behind you and he some zombies too the ground.

Then one of them torn his pant and try to bite the side of back and he push the zombies. he didn't know what to tells Jamie but he was very silent about what happened in the barn but she notice that he was like walking on the side and likes hurt and Jamie said what happened in the barn? Well I got attack by zombies, well did get bitten, I think I did, I have told you not too go and I did warn you that it was danger out there and you never listens to me and now they smell the fresh blood from you. And they will enter and eaten us up and they know that we are alive and now we have no escape and now we are trapped and will gets killed. Stop saying that's and run for your life and then we can make out of here from the farm house and then we can reach the road and head south of the mountain and go toward Canada and is that a good idea, I think better than saying here, that is true, yep.

Comes don't stall just keep on going and don't think the zombies can run that fast and I am too tired and then I just know that we have a chance but these zombies are much slower than the one that we ran into New Hampshire and I think they are the slower one but more hungry one and that want more brains and guts and whatever they are hungry for.

That is true, but I just don't this situation and then Jamie was grab and bitten and said Jack said no, and he cried out and yelled why did you hurt my love and she mean so much too me and now, Jamie will be part of them, I don't believe what just happened to her and I cannot looked at her, she is pale and some part are missing and slaughter in the street and I don't want to me next so I need to move faster and then he just fell on the rock and then three zombies pulled his hair and took a bite of his head and then he was dead and then a moment later, Jack got up and Jamie got up roaming the street.

Jack was following her likes a puppy dog even thought they were dead and Jack was still attractive to Jamie and then they saw some peoples walking the street and they grabbed them and bite them and torn them apart.

Moon eclipse, Day of Darkness

Book of Zombies

History of Zombies

Once upon a time there were Joy and April stumble through a lab in New Mexico and they find a book about the history how the zombies species got born and Joy said well we know there are thousand of zombies out there and now we need to figure out how to destroy them and April said well here is a book how they were make and well is there instruction about how to killed them, I am not sure but I don't want to be bitten, you won't and we will get out of this building, so we need to escape from the fire escape stairs and I think that they will not sees us and well if we stay we will be doom and I do wants to looks at the book now and who was the doctor that who was the one make those species and then we will killed them and then Joy went to the basement of the building and meanwhile Joy stay upstairs and then decided to sees what taking so long to with April but Joy knew that she had some obstacle to go through the building to reach her friend to the basement and then she saw the cages and over hundred of zombies locked up and one of them try to catch her and she ran quickly toward to April and then she called out her name and no answer and Joy had a fear that her friend was dead and then she saw her checking the files and Joy got a bit angry at April and said I wants to see them paper and then April said wait a minute, but I do know the medical logic, oh you think that I am stupid, no I am not, stop talking passed it too me now, and she grab her hand and almost fell in the sews and why are so mean too me? I don't know what you are talking about, yes you do and you wants to be the smart one but you are not.

Okay but too busy and I think at this point we should work together and not against each others and I think that we should have a plan and we know about the book and I think that we are not safe and I think if they know they will killed us and then get rid of the evidences, that is a possibility and I think that they could be watching us, nope not!

I think someone is behind the window and spying on us and you will tried to capture us and tried not to tell the truth and the book that will make the world chaos and panic, but so does it tell how they tested the volunteer with the virus and how long did it spread and there is no detail how it alls started with the homeless and then persons started to be missing and then one got escape and one zombies, spread the virus and then more persons became infection and then it spread others and person and it got out of control and they didn't capture that doctor with that antidote, nope and he is hiding out but now we have the possession of the book and we can be in danger and then we need to hide it and then minute later, Will and Ted came in and Joy said how did you comes in well the door was open and few zombies were trying to gets inside and then we shut the door,, I think so far we are safe, but I know that we cannot stay here and we need to leave and so what do you have in your hand, well let me sees, no it is my book and you cannot sees it but why, then somehow he just grab it from Joy hand and said.

Then Will said I think belong to my family and Joy said I wants it back no, and you are right we need to leaves, you don't know this place, so tell me about it well it is about there are thousand of zombies still locked up in the basement and I got feeling that they will break out and there are few walking around in the hall. You are saying that they are roaming the hall and they can attack any moment? Yep! Okay I am ready to leave and I wants to go now and we need to destroy the evidence, but why it tell you how to killed the zombies, well I don't want that my uncle were end up in prison and so I need to burn this book, no, I need to read though it now, if we wants to survive this epidemic, well you cannot and then he pushed her to the floor and then, then April came up to him and knock him and then she was pushed down and then he cover the face and tried to choke her and April grab him and said leave my friend alone and she pull her up and said hand over the book now, April then got her hair pull and then Joy tried to hit him in the head and then Ted said, stops this we are going to died if we don't stop fighting, well also I am taking this book and we will not give too you, do you understand if the government got the hold of this book, would use it against us, no I don't believe that's you must be envy but I am not, stupid

Then Ted said to Will what are we going to do about the book? I don't know but I don't want Joy and April too keeps it, so we will steal it from them. Yes went they are sleeping and then we will burned it, good plan I think so!

But about the "zombies" well we can just killed them off and there are not thousand of them but we will rid of them and we will find but the book might give us a clue where they are location and then we can just killed them, do you think that was the purpose of my uncle work to killed them I don't think he was using to get control and power so where is he now? I don't know but we better off without this book and we can become one like your uncle and I don't want no part of it, do you understand, Will said to Ted, well you are coward and I don't how I became your friend and so I am helping aren't I yes, and Ted said let do it and it will be over and then one of the April got up and said, don't let him destroy the book and it is very vital to save us from the zombies and if we do gets rid of the book, we might dies, don't listens to her and we will be fine and I know how to get out of here, we can be surrounded by the zombies and end being dead meat. No we will not so we are keeping the book, no but we are destroying it right now, and somehow Joy find a gun and said drop that book , or I will shoot you, you will not shoot me, try me., and Joy was not afraid to use the gun on Ted and Will said this broad is crazy and I am not going to stop her, Ted said you are chicken shit and I don't stand by me, you shit head, stop calling me names to Will,, you are, but I am shit head, or a jerk like you are. You might be taking ours chances, of living and not dying.

Destroy the evidence about zombies

Will said you about to threw the book into the fireplace and Will grab the book, and he ran but he couldn't go far zombies would behind.

Then Ted said called out and went to help him and Joy and April stayed inside and locked the door behind them and April said Joy we should go out and helped them, what to get killed, I don't think so, I am not going, you are staying alone, yes I am. Joy went out and looked around for the guys and they wouldn't not around, then Joy took the elevator at first it wouldn't work , and then it did and she would push the down button and got off and notice blood on floor and then saw the zombies were coming toward me and I just back up and push the button up and there were so near but that moment I step inside and the door close and went up and then I got off and then I heard April screaming they are inside they are trying to bite me, don't gets bitten, I am trying not too. One second Joy got a gun and blasted the zombies and they both safe for a moment, meanwhile Will and Ted would trying to hide into the air shaft and the zombies would trying to get inside and they block with a wood. But they broken the wood and got inside the shaft and grabbing there legs, one of zombie pull him and Ted try to get him back and it was too late for him and he kept going and didn't know what to do. Now what? I am alone but I still have the evidence and I will know what to do to get rid of the zombies by keeping the book in my possession. I will not perish in the epidemic and I will make it alive.

April and Joy said he is the vent and he wants to escape and get rid of the evidence and we need that book and it tells us how to tell the zombies, well I don't know but we need to find him now and then we will be okay!

Now do you know that we will I don't be Ted is the key of what happening around us and need to stops it and now the solution it find Ted and Will and take that book back and then we will be safe, because of the book , yes but why? It going to tells us " how to killed a zombies" well we do need a weapons to do so and do sees any weapons here but only zombies. you right but first we find the guys and then we will find the weapons and then we can escape from this place in one pieces I agree with you and about two minutes later they heard someone calling out for help and it Ted and in is in the air vent, at that moment that April climb inside the vent and then when through and search for Ted and then meanwhile Joy waited out and being patience and then she saw the zombies coming closer, so she called out and said I am a sitting duck so I am inside the vent too, and April said don't they are inside here too and it is a small space and I don't know if I am going to make it but then she spotted the book and was about to take it, Ted knock her out and when further into the wall and it seems long and so Joy climb in and crawl on her body and reach April and her head was dripping with blood and then she saw Ted and grab his leg and took out a gun and said hand it over now or I will shoot and he laughed at her and then she fire a shot and he surrender the book and she said why did you hurt her? Well, I had no choice but you know that this book is very important and so it cannot be destroy do you understand, I am not going to give to anyone but just safe keeping and you don't have to worry about your uncle, how do I know if you would change your mind, I might and do you sees any authority around? No and you are right but I need to find " Uncle Ben" but why he know the secrets of the zombies and he were tells us what kind of drugs were use on the human testing, well I don't like that there was human testing here and probably a lot zombies might be on the lose and my friend Will got venous by them and I almost got caught but I got lucky and I escape, and I think we should get out the vent and go out from the front door and find a car and leave.

So who is " Uncle Ben" well my mother brother that was a doctor that test on human species and it was very secretly then this happened !! then the epidemic and my uncle was missing and no one cannot find him so, maybe the zombies got him but I am not sure at this time, so they climb out and Joy hold on the book like a bible but they looked both ways and then they took the elevator to the lobby and walks out of the building and then Ted said I forgot something in the building and I will be right back, I am not letting you go back inside, yes I am it is important wait for me five minute and then if I don't comes out just leave, are you going to killed yourself if you go inside and that is suicide, no I am not but I need to looked, so don't fight with me right now, go it is safe now, we will wait, if the zombies comes, you drive away and don't look back, we are going with you, well you are so stubborn and April said I am not going back inside, and Joy said, you are chicken shit, well if the zombie come we will be dead meat no thanks! Joy said to Ted don't be long, I won't! but it might be a while so, just go! I don't wants to worry about you too, well fine and they got into Pontiac firebird and they drove away with the book and Ted was left behind and about two hours later, he was venous by the zombies and the girl were headed back to Manhattan, New York and Joy said I hope that he make it out, I don't think so, I think that the zombies got him, well that is a ashamed, I know he was hot and sexy but now we are once again alone headed to a unknown city that could be swamped by zombies but we have the book but we only got a pistol and with three bullets left,, we are not going make it too, I don't wants to hear that negative from you and I won't say it anymore.

So how many miles do have to Manhattan and Joy said probably over one hundred miles and then they stop at the gas station and there is no attendance, at the pump, well this is a self service, okay! I forgot that time had change and now you have to do this on your own.

That's true and also we are dealing with zombies and now the world could be ending and so we gets free gas, and free foods, but hope that we don't end being the chain food, if we are we cannot do anything but except what going on well I don't like this but we have no choice in the matter, so read the book and we need the I Q about the zombies, well they can be smart one but probably dumb one too, but they know how to survive. Help it does give you tips but there is a downfall in this book and two pages were remove, what Ted remove it, I think he did. But not so are we going back, no we are not so we need to find a more weapons, yes to shoot the zombies, that is the plan, well let get ready and we will beat, and we will killed them, and sure don't to be dead meat, we will not, now what I don't know but just keeps on moving, and we will win, so how did gets the confidence well, you the strong one.

Joy said stops the car, and got out of car what are you going? Just looking around and I think it clear and there is food store and I wants to grab some foods and bottle of water, but April said watched out, I will I will not be long, I can go inside and help you, I am fine. But April was sitting in car and resting and meanwhile Joy ran into the couple zombies in the store and trapped, Joy yelled out but April didn't hears her and Joy struggle with zombies, and now she is corner, and no escape. Then April sees and ran into the store with baseball bat and the pistol in her hand, and open the door wide and then knock down and pull her on the side and then they both ran outside got into the car and drove away.

Then April yelled at her and don't do this again! I won't I promise, on our lives, do not sacrifice our lives and I want to live, fine and we can deal with anything, yes we will. Yes I do. But focus on the road and no more stops, but if we need to use the restroom, we will do it. It was getting dark and it was after midnight, and Joy said where did you hide the book, underneath the seat, oh that good, so let keeps driving I am don't be a dictator, no I am not, yes you are sometime thanks! Then April got silent and then looks out of car and seem clear from zombies.

The remains

Then they came upon the street and they saw the zombies are coming toward us, now what? We just keeps going yes right through, good don't let them get near the car, I won't. so tells me how it alls started in the lab in the hospital and then they started to killed off the patience and then they gave them a shot and they wake them up and then they became zombies, well that is the history of the zombies, but looks at them and there bodies are opens up and you sees there guts and body parts, yes they are the experiment from the lab and they lost control and they were in populations and I cannot believe that there were human subject that they went into routine lab rat for medical research and mistake in surgery and wake up the dead with the needle with some break out through, but a error occur, and it cause some reaction and make the subject to go out the brain,, because have a craving for brains and stopping to hurt, but the record show that they are dead that are the walking dead. But they would control by getting shot to stops the urge for brains but sometime it doesn't work, sometime the procedure sometime fail, okay I don't wants to hears what happens but what going on now, well we trapped between the living and the dead, huh, that is true but we cannot stand here in the middle of street, the zombies roaming the street and we are sitting like ducks, sure we are and manage to escape from here, but we cannot, we need gets the hell out of here and find survivor and not end up the street and they were so progressive and aggressive that they mean that they need the brains for the brains to stop for pain to stops and zombies, coming what are we going to do? Well run from here and find a place to hide but where? We are in open and they are coming fast and I don't know but they are. Just don't stand there move, yes I am. Then April said I will go inside the bar and grill and make sure no one in there. I will be careful and April went inside and called out to Joy.

April came out and was like off balance and almost fell down to the ground, no you are not a zombie? Then she looked closer to her face and she was drooling from here mouth, no April you are a zombie, but why did you get bitten, and she grunt and wanted to bite Joy. Joy started to cried and said now I am alone, now I loss my dear friend, Joy walks away before that's she put a stick into her head and she was gone, and got into the car drove away and before that she took the bracelet from her hand and it was a charms of there friendship and put into the gulf department, and cried all days for her friend April, and stop and I hate being alone and I wants my friend back, I need to go back and gets her, so am I crazy? Now I am talking to myself.

Joy got out the car and really not seeing what coming forward but then looks they were about inch away, then one zombie try to bit her, so that moment she pull her arm away and then I started to run and run and I was out of breath and then he was standing there and then he grab her and got inside and said he said, gee I am glad too meet you, who are you? Tony nice too meet you, and what is your name, my name is Joy and I thought I was a goner, but you are not because I am here, well Tony how do we get the hell out of here? Well we don't we stay and wait until morning and then we will headed southwest, I heard on the report that the west coast is not infection with the zombies and that is a relief and I know but first we need to get out of here first, that is true, and I sees you were crying, yes I was I lost my best friend of this epidemic and I hate this awful situation and I just don't like it and I don't know who cause it? I don't know but we will leave this place in the morning and then we will be safe I hope, but there are no guarantees in life and the saying sooner or later you do died but not in a tragedy ways that is true but we will figure out how to make it alive and then we can go to Los Angeles, is that a good place for now, I think so. But not sure at this moment they are breaking inside, yes they are coming!

The zombies are breaking in!!!

Hold them back, and I am trying my best when I tell you to run, you run do you understand I am not leaving you.

We need to leaves immediately and we will not catch us and they will eat us up and eat and eat and we will be gone and I don't like this scenario and I think that we better go now, sure I do agree with you totally, okay let go! What are you waiting for? I don't know but longer we stay the less chance of getting out, I know said Tony to Joy and it will be a difficult task and I thought that we will be able to pull it off and I hope so because I don't wants to be static and I do wants to survive this so do I and I think that we will be able to escape and I like that idea, so do I. later that night Tony looked around and said well they are still here but we can just fight them if and then get into the car and Joy said well I don't think so because the car is out of gas and that why I stops driving so I think that we are stuck here and I think that we should hide in the freezer and then Joy said how will we get out if it locked, well then we freeze, I don't like that's well what other solution do have, you just have a pistol with three bullets and that will not help us out, unless we use if for ourselves and well I don't want to killed myself I just wants to live when the epidemic is over and I don't know when that will happened? But we need to be positive do you understand? Yes but that will not killed the zombies so near that they smell us and wants to chew down on us we are there food supplies, I don't wants to hears that's but you must, why don't you just shut up and let me think of a plan to get out of here, well we can walks out but we will be slaughter, and that we would be awful and I think were be terrible, yes and I think that someone out there will rescue us, stop dreaming,, no but

I don't wants to stay here, I don't neither, but right now we have no choice in the matter.

But Joy was a bit eager to leaves and she thought maybe she could just sneak out and Tony were not notice and that she thought to herself and then said what a bad idea and I will stick with Tony and I will be safe with him. Meanwhile Tony said there is a back room and I think it is solid and it will hold us and prevent the zombies getting us, so you so brilliant and I am glad that I am not alone and with you. Well it just started to rain and it is like acid rain and I think that you are right and I think there will be more zombies in the morning and I hope not but it is true and it make the zombies population to grows but we need to find a window and get out of here and find a car and drive away and not too looked back, your right, I know.

Well, I believe that we will gets along and I like that, the only reason that I am agreeing is staying alive, well so far we are and soon has they break inside and we will be goner, stop saying that Tony. It was about midnight and Joy looked out and seems they were gone and so she open the door and then Tony said are you nuts you know that you could have let them in if I didn't shut the door, looks how many out there? I sees them now but I am sorry but I just wanted to looked and smell the fresh air and so I just got a bit careless, sorry, don't apologize but you did put us in danger, yes I will not do that again, promise that you won't! I promise Tony on my life, and he smiled, well we still could loss ours lives and so we are not out of the woods so we just have to keeps ours eyes open and be alert whatever happened and I think we should tried attempt to escape and not being caught and so I know the drill and let do it before they multiply in numbers I agree when I count to ten and we run out there and keep running and make sure that they don't catch you but it is raining hard but so what. That is a distract and I think it will work and tried to get the end of the road and keep going straight and I will be in back of you, will you be in back of me? Yes I will be, I promise, I never lies, can I trust you? Yes!

Acid Rain

Joy and Tony ran out and the rain and I don't like how the rain is falling on my head and I think that we will get infection and Tony said now you are acting paranoid, no I am not but it is getting me weak, that ails in your mind, Joy, no it is not and I just wants to go back inside before we turned into zombies. you must be ridicules, no I am not and I just don't like being in this kind of situation and well you need to deal with life and what going on and so we just have move on and found a safe place to stay and it is not here and I am sure that we will find it. well so should we just stop in the middle of the street and let them gets us? No I don't think so we just need to run and run and gets away from the zombies, yes and no and because they are everywhere, that is true but maybe less population and but still got to shoot them and we don't have weapon so we need to find a gun shop and bullets, fine. Well we are going into that area and we stock up and be ready for the envy and we will not lose focus and we will not died unless we get careless and then we will not make it, do you hears what I am saying too you Joy, well I loss my friends I know exactly what you saying and don't called me stupid I am not but you could be a dumb blonde, thanks a lot and I save your ass so many times that you don't even appreciate me.

Well, I wants to says that you are not that bright and you were be dead if I didn't step in when I came along that probably not true, but don't denied it and you it is,, well I am not liar and I make it this fast without you, so if I left toady, you were be alone and maybe dead, I don't like your sarcasm and you acting like a jerk, thanks a lot and next time I will not be there for you, promises and I don't want your helped, fine, I am going and I believe that you will not make, you need me, that is bull and Tony walks out and Joy stayed inside, and said you are risking ours lives because you are selfish, no I am not and you are a such a bitch, thanks, no I am not.

Meanwhile the rain was falling and it felt like radioactive that was affect the zombies population and then, Tony started to sneeze and cough and blood was coming out of his mouth, and snagging and back and forward and was a bit like a grunt and drool and acting like a zombie and at this time I shut the door tight and I was frighten that he probably have the key to get inside and now I just was sitting at the door and handing my hand together and it was like a pray, and now he came to the door and banged on it hard and hard at that moment it was about too open so I ran into the other room and shut it tight, but I knew that he knew where I was to hide and I know I had to leaves this place now. It is was getting darker and darker and I couldn't sees where he was and now I really was scare that I was going to died in this place and I looks out of the window and there were thousand and thousand and then, I know that I had to run and get into the firebird and drove away but they still follow me and I didn't k now the areas so I just kept on driving and until I knew I was out of that city. At that moment I didn't slow down but I just sped away and make sure that I would hit a lot of zombies way out and I was not thinking straight but I knew I had to get the hell out of there now, and I ran a red light and I didn't looks if anyone was crossing the street, like a person and then I thought they are dead and I would not get in any trouble, and there were no police but everything was like chaos and then I was out but was safe but I need to find a place to stay until I can travel during day and the storm was getting more thunder and lighting and the only thing that I saws was is zombies everywhere and I stop suddenly and almost, ran into the ditch and the car was stuck in the mud and then I thought how the hell will I get out of here and they are coming what will I do, and somehow hid behind the tree and bushes but I was still seen by zombies and now I was terrify and I didn't know what to do, then I saw the house and now I knew that I had to go there now!

House of Zombies

Joy stood there for a while and at first I thought I were run but I didn't want to gets notice, so I walks very slowly but also thought it was stupid but I was not sure what I was going to run into, so I just walk inside and I didn't realize that I was in the house of zombies and they were very vicious and hungry and I just stood like a piece of meat and I just knew that I need to escape I knew that they smell me and I was going to become a zombie. That was my nightmare that were come true. Also I thought to myself why did I go inside and I were been safer out then here, and they started to sniff me and try to grab me and now I was not about to be chew up by them. One of the zombies seem a somewhat similar of old friend but he was the first one that wanted to take a piece of me and I refuse to be "dead meat" and so I somehow kick him down and I ran out and somehow I tumble into dozen of zombies and they were very suspicious and they were more advance and much quicker and I didn't like too deal with that scenario and so I somehow knock him down and about three of them came toward me and somehow I manage to get the gun and shot a few and ran into the woods and then I saw the little girl crying and I was about to go up too her and about minutes later she was venous by the hungry zombies, and I still watched and but I didn't wanted to be the target and I ran and ran for my lives and then I saw a car coming and I try to tag it down but it were not stops and I was getting tired and wet and so I just ran, and then I fell into some trap, that I was surrounded by zombies, but I pull out there hair and hit them over the head and they fell down and I pick up a rock and I hit there skull and they were dead I thought the crisis were over but I was mistaking and I just had to fight for my live and until, I was save by a man and he was very nice and took me into his car and drove me out from there, and he warns me that no not go back to the house of zombies, and I didn't asked why?

There are many mores zombies coming and I don't know if we will be able to gets way from here and I don't wants think about that right now, just keeps on running and you will be safe and I will be in back of you and don't worry about it, I am and I don't likes being chase by the undead and they wants my brains, I know that is there foods and we are there supplies.

But keeps on running and we will get out of the house of zombies and go toward the left of the house and get into that boat and sail away from and that is not really that close to us and I think that we might not make it, why are being negative and I don't wants to hears anymore that's do you understand Joy said Tony, how you acting like a jerk,, well with you, you rub ,me the wrong ways, so we don't get together because you are like poison too me, thanks, I save your ass so many times that, I shouldn't let the zombie gets you, well I will be in your ways again! So you will go on your ways, good luck, you will need it, thanks a lot. But are we going to be able to be safe and I don't know how to answers that Joy but we should talked about it but just go and I think that you right so keeps on moving and don't let them sees you fine, they won't how do you know, they are staring at us and they will be following us and then we will be dead like a door nail and then we will become a zombie, stop staying that's and I don't like being in this situation and the scenario it does not seem good, I know, just keeps running into the woods, I will be slam into them there too, just don't let them catch you, I won't you do the same, okay! Joy and Tony ran into the woods and then they were partial safe but more zombies were coming from alls directions from the woods and even from the house of zombies, and it is a very danger and lay low and behind the bushes, okay! About a minute later, Joy thought she was clear but she ran into more zombies near the lakes, and Tony ran into them toward the graveyard, and now they both were stuck.

Joy was about to called out to Tony but they grab him into the woods.

Ah! Zombies, Ah! Zombies Dogs coming this ways!

Joy called out to Tony but he didn't answer not at alls and at this moment she knew that she was alone, and Joy walks and walks toward the dirt road and know one came by and it was really cold and windy and Joy knew she needed to go into somebody house for shelter but there were no houses in sight but only graveyard that zombies were climbing out and then Joy turned into the corner, there were dogs, and they were zombies and they wanted to bite her and Joy took a stick and poke the zombie dog to death and there were mere coming her way! Now Joy knew that she was not going to make it but Joy decided to hide in the grave, and thought it were be a good idea but then thought probably were gets bitten sooner by the zombies, and changes her mind and headed north and the intersection and head toward Maine.

The dogs would chasing at me, what will I do, I don't I cannot stops they will bite me, I will be dead, I will gets the infection and I will end up dead I will keeps on running, and I hide but they will be scent and they catch me, no I need to find water, but they could be the water, but I need to take chances, if I don't know I will be dead meat. At this I was breathless and barely too walks, they are getting closer, I thought at that moment I would be goner, and they chase a cat and grab it and ate the cat and chew it up and watching me, at that moment they would staring at me, I thought I was going to died but then my hero came with a fast car and drove through the bushes and branches and called out and I looked and it was man with a red jeep and I steps inside he said my name is Tom.

Nice too meet you, you came at the right time and you save me, thanks! Otherwise I would be dead meat, so you, I need says your lifesaver and I would stuck in the woods and probably, would end dead…

Tom said I came from the New Jersey and there a slight problem.

I don't know understand, what your saying, well there is crisis.

So what is the lately news about the epidemic, well not that good, what do mean not so good? Well, zombies are growing by the minute, and it is not safe to walks alone in the street because you were gets swamped by zombies,, well it is in every town in the east coast that the special report, and to be careful and caution how you are walking and severe precaution, that is the special alert, well it does not sound good, nope it is not!!! So where should go? Well probably toward Texas and west coast will be safe and we will not runs into zombies and we will be fine and we will sees other peoples that are undead that they are walking and they will be just likes us, I think I heard that story before and I do have some doubt about going there but maybe you right, Tom so I don't want to stay here in the woods with hungry zombies, so let go now and I do know where is a gas station that I can filled up the car with gas? No I am not from this area, I just got lost in the woods and I am glad that you came and now we can leaves this terrible place, I agree but the jeep doesn't have too much cover and we have too be careful because the zombies will grab us and we have no protection,, yes I know and you can drives much quicker than the zombies move? Yes I know so, I am ready and let go!!! They both got inside the jeep and drive and drive into the dirt road and out of the wildness and no sight of anyone, and alone in the woods and so how far are we before we leave this territory, about twenty minutes or more and not sure, well I cannot wait until we get on the highway and head toward Texas and do know if this epidemic and I think that we will make it and that ways they will not smell our scent and so farther we gets the better and than we will run into some problem but not sure what kind but be prepare and then we will be totally safe, are you sure? Yes I am and I cannot wait but we need to get some water and guns and bullets and grenades and supplies making bomb, even some fireworks but why?

Well that is the distract and that will help us to escape from here.

Escape from Zombies

Now it will be a difficult task and then we will have find some electric power to shut down and then we can get into the military bases and then we can gets missiles and anything that we find that will be good of killing off the zombies on the ways, but now you are scaring me, but why? Because you said that we need that kind of supplies, well that is survivor, and then we can travel safety to Texas, there is a other reason of running into zombies, so it is better to prepare and likes for any kind of storm, well you saying, yes I was thinking of good escape plan and not too runs into zombies.

Well there is no plan because somehow the zombies attack we need to be ready, we need to be guard and then we need to this zone and to be safe and I don't know what we might run into and then we will be fine so far. Hope that your right! Travels and be safe and getting out of here, and making it is too difficult, and I don't know but we are taking a risk and then we will be to a safe zone, is there one? I think so and but things are changing and I think that we should be just quiet and then we can sneak into the Texas and then we will be safe, okay said Tom too Joy and you sound like you're a new Yorker, how do you know because you so rude and selfish so that how I know well,, you have too be tough in New York because they were chew up and spite you out, oh I sees, tough lady, well not really but you sure do act it, maybe I do and I don't wants to be like a floor mat that you can walks all over me, well I won't my princess, stop calling me princess, I can fight like a man and so I am your equal, well I don't think so you only about one hundred and five pound and I am more stronger and not weak like you so I don't need the insult from you, well stop chatting and listen what I am saying if we make out we will be lucky and I think that we are surrounded around us and I need to figure out how to get the hell out of here.

Any suggest from you, well you called me the weakly so I don't know what to says, I will says I will be quiet and I will sees what you will plan it out and if I agree and it works out then we will be alive, good plan.

Meanwhile the sun was going down and it was silver moon and Joy looks up and then said I think it is time that we just move out and I think it is safe now, so how do you know? Well the moon give us light and that is the sign to move, well I will go along with that's right now but remember we need to stop and rest and if you don't we will end up at a ditch,, and then the zombies will eat us up. Joy didn't really didn't wants listen to his advice but she know that she had no choice in the matter, so Joy just lay back and fell asleep and then Tom got out his phone and called up a friend and said we are headed your ways and I have a lady friend with me, and then he hang up the phone and kept driving, and then stops and got out and his friend came to him and said come with me to the barn, about her, just let sleep, I have something to show you, and then his friend open up the barn and said Tom said you have walker, yes I do and then he shut the door behind him said they are infection humans, I know that, and they wants your brains, I know too, so what are you trying to tell me, well I think I know how not to catch it, so what is it? well not exactly sure but I am going to take this drug and it should not affect my brain, well what wrong with you? I think I have the virus,, what and you giving it too me I should just shoot you in the head now, well not exactly but I just feel I have some kind of bug, and Tom was going to pull the trigger on Tim, and that moment Joy ran out of the car and said you left me here alone and I could been eaten up and you are talking with your friend and I was nor protection and you are a jerk.

Come on stop calling me names girly, don't called me girly I should slapped you on your face, well I would like too sees it, well then Tom pull his hand and back and said this is my friend Tim and nice too meet you, same here!

Heading to Texas zone free of Zombies

When they headed to Texas and the road a lot debris and a lot of body parts and then bloods stains and zombies everywhere is no escape but out of Vermont and Maine and New Hampshire and not in Manhattan but head south and we will be safe but we need to gets out the zombies zone and we will be fine, but when we will leaves this areas and keeps going south and then we is that good but we are not in the clear but we still have a small chance to gets out of here and have a normal lives and gets infection and not get bitten, and so I like that you are taking me away from here and I will tried to contact one of my friends and maybe they are not illness from this terrible situation that I was been in and you got me out and I really appreciate me and I don't know how to repaid you for helping me and well, kindness of my heart stay alive, I will and so how many away I don't know but we have a lot to through before we are safe, and at this moment we are still in the danger zone and don't let them hears you, I won't! I promise but don't let them sees you, they can smell you and they will comes toward us and I cannot beat them off by myself, and I will help you out but there are too many of them don't you get it, sure I do but we cannot just sit here like sitting ducks and they will venous us and we will be dead meat that for sure, and we don't have protection and they are able to get inside because the jeep is easy access and we are still in danger,, yes and I know but just keeps driving and then we will be out of here and I don't know what we will run in Alabama, but sure we will be okay and I also have to stop for gas and don't walks too far from the car I won't and don't you hears a sirens, yep!

It is really loud and it is a warning and I think that sound that the zombies are on the lose and we are in the middle and so we have a problem and the road that we drove in they are standing around it and we have no way out, and you must be kidding but I am not.

Joy got really terrify ands said you said that we are going to safe and now you put me into danger, thanks a lot, and I don't need the stressed but I just want to get the hell out of here immediately, well you didn't started the engine and we are still in the opens are you crazy, girly and don't called me that,, well I thought we were be fine and now we are going to be dead meat, well it will be Alabama, and we will be headed to New Orleans and then toward to Texas and then we can rest and then we can head to Texas but we need to hear the news about zombies, so what are they saying, well to go inside and not be near one, the world is going chaos, that is true. So what will we do? Just head to Texas and don't listen to the special report and but that is important, if we don't we could end up dead that true but we stay we still could died,, well moving is and but they know that we are here that great, so they are really advance and so they are more quicker, well that sucks and we are not far like those zombies, but I am not giving up on my live no matter what? Do you hears what I am saying? I sure do and I do like the guts that you have and I am glad to be with you, and thanks for not leaving me behind, well I would not leave you neither, and then Tom kissed her lisps and Joy said why did you do that's because I am attractive to you, I feel the same about you, but we cannot get serious right now but we need to think of survive this ordeal and then we will try some day to have a relation, I know, what you means, yeah I do! Just keeps going and I will be quiet like a mouse, that is good, and then Tom put the radio and Joy said you wants them to hears us? No but we need to know how far it spread, yes the virus, yes and not to get into the middle of the epidemic, and the world is going crazy and the hospital turning into morgue and I don't know what went wrong, I don't neither, I just when out and now I am trying to find my home and everyone is missing and I don't know if I will ever sees them again, I know. Now what? Got a flat tire, great!

Moon Eclipse, Day of darkness

Ambush by Zombies!

Ambush

Tom and Joy ended on a detour and Tom was getting upset and not patience at alls and didn't wants to tells her that they are trapped and there is no escape and but right now, Tom was very quiet and didn't want her to panic and alert the zombies of the location and then Joy said how many miles do have to go? Tom nodded his head and said I am not sure but we will get there soon, and then Joy said you are not telling me everything,. Well I like to keep thing to myself and is that alls right? Well if concern my welfare I should know, once again you are right but don't panic, why? Do you sees them? Yes I do! They are around us and I just when the wrong ways and I think , that I will not be able to gets out of this, I don't understand what you are saying but you need us to gets ways now. I don't wants to get any attention from the zombies and they are really fast and advance and they will chew us up and spit us out, and they are vicious and very, very danger, that I know I did fight with a few of them, there was a point that they were going to gets me but somehow I got lucky and I escape and the second time was when you rescue me and took me into your car and we drove away, yes I do remember that incident, it was recent and you were not that fast.

Thanks a lot Tom, but I did save your ass a lot of times too and you are not just the hero and you were also the victim and I think we helped each others and still together and in this case,. We don't have a good chance, and then we will survive this epidemic, I believe you and I am just frighten and scare and I don't wants to screw up and be eaten by the zombies and I do hears you and don't worry about it, I am for you and I know you for me. So we will be save together and not to wander off and I do not wants to be alone I don't neither, just listens what I am saying and you will be safe, but they do smelled us and I don't wants to be caught, stay in the car and be quiet and don't put on the radio, I won't!

They are coming closer and closer and so start up the car and it won't start and I don't know what to do? The engine can be flooded and I think tried to start it up again, and about a three minutes later, they somehow they drove away and then now Joy was relief so was Tom and Joy said don't put us in this situation, but we are still not out of the woods and we still have zombies around us, I know but we will gets out, but looked at the gas tank, it almost empty, that is not good, I know I think that we have to walks out here, with so many zombies, that is not possible but we will do, I just believe, what words I am saying and we will make it through the ordeal of the nightmare of this virus, yes I know but I am still worry and hungry and don't get bitten or get the drool from the zombie, because you will be one, no I will not let it happen and I will just do what you says and I will keeps us safe, you can take my word , said Joy too Tom I likes to hears that but then the car stall and then Tom said now we have to run and run for our lives, and don't let back I will be behind you and don't worry, we will make it, I believe you, Tom and then Joy somehow trip over the rock and fell on the ground and then Tom pick her up and said are you alls right? Yes and they ran and ran and then Joy said I cannot run anymore but I need to rest, not right now, but a little further away and then we can rest, fine, if I need to carry you I will, I will be fine, I am exhaust and I am very hungry, well we are in the woods of Alabama. And we are far from Texas so we will have to hike and get there somehow, well I got it and don't worry I will keep up with you and I will not give up on life, but Tom was not telling her that he was a hurt and in pain but didn't want to scare her that he might be infection and Tom was holding the guns and bullets and then he stop and said now it seem to be clear, and we can stop here for a while and about a minute later, Joy notice that Tom was bleeding and said why are you keeps it from me? Well I didn't want to tell you, I said no secrets, do you understand? Yes, I do.

Tom and Joy stops for a while and then Joy said I wants to looked at that wound and Tom said it is fine, and Joy looked and said well it looks like it swollen and red and infection, but why didn't tell me I would have clean it up, well I just wanted to keeps on going, well seem like you didn't care about yourself I do and I do care for you too, I know that why you kept it quiet not to get me into a panic attack that true and I cannot denied what I am doing and I just want us to make it to Texas and without the car it going to be longer and walking we will need to find a shelter and then move on in the morning, I know that but before we enter we need to check it out,, totally.

But don't get hurried if we sees the house, I will first go inside but I don't sees any property right now, well I don't neither, well we just keeps on walking and we will be fine, how do you know? I am just trying to be positive said Tom to Joy, so am I so I wants to lay down on a bed and sleep for couple hours, so do I. meanwhile Tom was looking around but they were going in circles and they were lost but he didn't wanted to tell Joy, they had a problem and then Joy saw about a hundred zombies and said we need to hide they are coming very close and they will sees us, no. hide in the bushes they spotted us so what do we do now? Get way now, I am but they are getting nearer and nearer and I don't like it but comes on just don't stand there, I am not but I need to go now. But they are getting closer, no, I don't believe it, what? You got bitten. No I have not, looked you bleeding, no the skin broke, don't lies too me tell me the truth, I am. No your not!

Then the rain came down and then Tom said I sees a cabin, that great, at this moment, I thought we were lost, in someway we were and you didn't tell me, well I didn't wanted to tell you, well once again you are keeping things from me, sorry, I am a loner, well I am not. So tell me about yourself not now, well you are a stranger that I trust and but I know you kept me safe, that is true, thanks!

Shelter surrounded by Zombies

Tom I sees it, what the cabin and can we go inside the rain is pouring hard I know but you need to follow the rule, I first go inside and check it out and then I will called you in, but I am not safe standing out here and I need to comes with you, well you are right! So comes on and don't make a sound I won't are sure and then she step inside and said seem like no one live here and so we can stay here until we are ready to go, on our journey., yep! I agree and then we can take these supplies and then we will not be hungry and but we cannot let the zombies that we are inside, I know that's! I am not stupid, and I will be careful. Meanwhile Tom when outside and Tom called out, we have a generation and it will keeps the lights on and then we can listen to the TV, and also I will check the cellar, but I will go with you, good, I will be behind you, sure...

Tom got some wood for the fireplace and then brought it in and then I think I brought enough in and I think we will be fine, and also I will locked the windows and doors and then they will not get inside, that is great! But a minute later there was a banged at the door, they are here, we are surround, so do you have a escape plan, I didn't think about it, well I thought you did. Great! Don't be a pain I won't be so don't act like you're my boss but I am not, so I am trying to be patience with you but you are getting me mad and furious and you don't listens what I am saying and I don't know that we make it so far and you are making me sick, I would leaves but I cannot because the what going in the world, I know, well I trying so badly but I cannot help it but is this really scaring and I need someone to tell me that everything will be okay, I cannot because they are out there and waiting to eat us up, so I cannot tell you different, well so what do we do mean while? Wait until morning and maybe we can leave quietly and then get to Texas, and more rain fell and mores zombies came and now what?

I will looks out and you sleep and we will take shift and then we can gets some sleep and not to doze off, do you understand? Yes I do! So Joy when on the couch and lay down and turn off the lamp and slept and meanwhile, Tom looked out and then he heard a sound in the basement and then he thought to himself and said I am not going to check it out, and once again the window smash and then Tom got up and then opens the door and there were the zombies on the stairs and then Tom push the door against the feet and shut it tight, and he ran up to Joy said get up we need to leave now but Joy was half sleep and was still like sleeping and then once again he shake her and said get up now., okay what going on? They are in the cabin and in the basement and they will get us,. No move on now,. Fine let me put on my shoes, I will be ready in a minute I think you better be ready now.

I am trying and then Joy and Tom opened up the door and they were standing on the porch and Tom said count after 3 run into the woods, and Joy I hears you, and then Tom open the door and they both ran into the woods and knock down a few zombies on the ways and they follows them and now we are in the opens, but we need to hide in the bushes, I think that will works,, but they can smelled us, yes but if they get near just run and don't let them catch you, I won't! promise me if I get bitten you shoot me, and you do the same for me, I will don't hesitate, I won't Tom.

But please don't leave me behind if I just runs slow, don't worry I will wait for you, good, even though you rub me the wrong way. Thanks!

Tom and Joy ran and ran and then Tom and Joy were out of breathe, and Joy and Tom sat on top of the hill and looked around and no sight of the zombies at that time and now Joy and Tom were relief that they were safe, for now, but we should not stick around long here,, they might get our scent and get us, that is true, but it looked like it going to rain, your right and we will gets soaked if we don't get inside and any suggest Tom?

"Bright Lights"

Joy and Tom looked up and what was that lights? I don't know but it infection my eyes, mine too, so is this causing the virus? I don't know Joy but that was a mistake to looked at the lights, and now we will become zombies, don't says, we won't, now do you know, I don't know.

Once again, a flash in the light, don't looked it, another one, so what going.

We need to hide now, yes in hurried, they are coming and they sees us yep, they are very near and don't let them bite you, we are surrounded by zombies, and what are the chances of getting out very slim. Don't says that we were in a tougher situation and we got out and now you are giving up, no ways I am going to fight for my life and not died because the zombie, I like to hears that Joy, keep hiding and they are passing by us and they don't smelled us and don't make a sound, okay, and about a minute later, Tom sneeze and they heard it and they were approaching us and now we were trap and they the flashing lights continues and continues and more zombies were coming toward them, and now what? Runs, where they are everywhere, I cannot believe what going on here and you don't me not to make a sound and you did and now we are in trouble, thanks a lot. Don't act like a bitch we need do a distract and leave this areas, and I don't know if it going to works at this point of so many zombies, so one of us we need to sacrifice, well Joy will you be the bait and no I will not you were the one that make the sound and you would be the bait, thanks a lot when I save your sorry ass so many times before and you wants to died, no but I might help you to lives.

But I don't understand how, well you are the bait and when they are coming toward you I will step in and some out distract them and we both will be able to gets way, hope that your plan will work, I hope so!

But you are not so sure about the plan and seems like you have not sure about it, that you right about that's ! I don't like it, but we are wasting time. The time that we don't have and they are coming and we both might end of being dead, you are right so let do it and sees what happened and I will save you, I promise you with my life, fine. Those lights are flashing and it just kept on going and mores zombies are coming and I do think that the light have some effect? I think it does and I just don't wants to be around when they are vicious and hungry and I don't wants to be in the middle I don't neither I just wants to gets away from me so I do. So let go now, I am going and I am not stopping here, I am behind you but the lights is effect my eyes sight and I think don't looks at it, why? Just don't it really bad and I think just keeps walking and don't looks back and fine and they kept walking and walking and there was no end and then they stop end of the road and then Joy saw the house on the hill and then we will go there! is that a good ideas, yes it is and I think that we will hide out until we leave for Texas and then we will rest and then we will not looked at the light, I got it and so go inside and locked the door tight and the windows and but we didn't check inside, well we just taking a chance so we are probably be safe, I hope so, we will be all ready, we will be don't worry and we will survive this and we will sees our friends and then we will have ours lives back, you are so sure about that's? yes I am and I hope that you believe me, I will and don't worry and tomorrow we go and travels more and then we will not have too fight with the zombies and then the world will be the same, okay! That night Joy and Tom stick together and Joy didn't wants to shown him how scare she was but then Tom gave her a hug and kiss and then fell asleep in each other arms and the next morning Joy got up and make coffee and waffles and toast and Tom was surprise when he got up and said, I didn't know that you can cook , and he sat at the table and Joy join him and they had breakfast together and then said we will rest for awhile and then we will leave about one hour from now, good! I am happy, so am I .

The Long Journey unknown

J oy and Tom pack the bag with supplies and weapons and they were
ready to go back to the unknown origin and Joy was a bit afraid but
was brave to step out before Tom went out and Tom said wait for me,,
you don't wants to be trapped by zombies, I don't wants but I just want
my life back,, I agree with you and I don't know what happened out here
but it may not be everywhere, but we will be fine, I am glad that you are so
positive about this and I hope this over and we can go back to our family,
that might not be possible, I don't know when it going to happened but the
military is out there and we will be safe and then they will gets rid of the
zombies and the virus and we will make it alive, so you are so sure about it
and I am and so don't think otherwise we might be the last of the persons
alive on this planet, you don't says, well you don't believe me looked out
there and you will sees, and I am I only sees zombies roaming the earth
and we are in a nightmare that might never end, stops saying that's I don't
need this negative from you and I also don't wants to end up dead neither,
I agree with you totally ands stay behind and don't get lost in the middle
of the zombies, I won't! later that night Joy was not patience and she was
walking backward and forward that make Tom very mad, and then Joy
sat down in the car and we are on our ways and we will be dealing with a
lot of things that might comes up and don't be scare, I will protection you,
yeah, yeah, I heard that before and you think that I am joking but I am
not. Well we will be there in two days and maybe sooner and if we don't
run into zombies, much sooner so you have confidence, sure I do and you
should have the same I do.

When Tom was driving Joy fell asleep and so far the journey seems like
it was going fine, but then suddenly the car stall in the middle of highway

and Joy said, and then woke up and said what happened? We are swamped by zombies, so what are we going to do now? Runs has fast you can and don't looked back, and I hope that you do the same, I will not be dead meat for zombies, no ways in hell and just keeps running and I think that's near the border of Texas but this virus must have spread further, well I think that your right but just run and don't talked, fine! I am getting exhaust and I need to rest and not right now I do understand and I just need to have some water and someplace to sit that were be nice but not now!! Tom said loud and clear and Joy said okay, okay, I do hears you and they are really fast zombies, today I don't wants to died, just runs and I am.

At that moment, suddenly Joy stops and then was pulled into the web of zombies and screaming for help and Tom trying to rescue her and then Tom was trapped and couldn't gets too her, and then he was also trapped and then a motorcar came and pulled up and got Tom, and then Joy and then he said, well, well, more persons alive and I will take you to the camp and you will be examination by the doctor and have you been bitten? No I have not but sees need to be seen by the physician, is that a good idea? Yes and they can give you the right doze of the virus invention, I like to know is there a side effective. I don't know miss, and why are you so worry? Really I am not but I would like the precaution, I hears you! They drove about two miles down the road and they saw the camp surrounded by zombies, and electric fence and then I don't like this place, we will be like guinea pig here, don't let him hear you, well it is true, silent, fine, I don't know what we are in for but I do have a bad feeling about this place, well explains looked like they test on humans, what and then sir heard her and he said you are mistaking about that we tried to cure the sick and make them well, oh sorry about that's! then the motorcar stop in the compound and they were leading into the lab and they were tested and then were release, and into a hospital room and will be tested again, I don't like them poke me and I feel terrible about that sorry I got you into this but if he didn't comes, we were been dead.

End of the epidemic

Today will be release from this camp and you will be safe and to go anywhere you wants and Tom and Joy couldn't believe that they were going home again! is it really happening, yes it is and I am so happy about it and now I can go and sees my family if they survive this ordeal, they probably did.

At first Joy and Tom were afraid to steps out and so what happen to those zombies and they are alls gone, and now I feel better and now we are safe to walks the street and so how are we going to gets back to Manhattan? Well we can take the train and we can drive back, about your family well they live in New Jersey and they are probably gone with the blast of the nuclear bomb, that is awful, yes it is and there is no reason to get that missiles and killing innocence peoples about a mistake that took place and then persons turning into zombies and the government fault, yes they were trying to prevent the terrorist and they killed there own peoples and the virus spread, yes, that what happened, so long stories short, this is the end of the epidemic. And it is a relief, yes I do agree with you so I am heading back home and I am still going to Texas, to visit few cousins and aunts, I sees I will be traveling alone, so what do I do I run into zombies? you won't! it is over, are you sure? Yes, hope that you are right and hope that they are gone, but I still have that bad feeling in my stomach, well maybe something that you ate. Yes and I know it is not over but once again someone is lying to us and who do you means? Well the government, I knew that but think that your right but I don't wants to says anything else, someone might just listen what we are saying, okay! But don't get paranoid, I won't.

Later that day, Joy when to the train station and got a ticket and waited for the train to comes and there were not a lot of persons around but still had some fear that Joy would runs into zombies, and then it was time to aboard the train and then Joy when into the seat near the door,, in case a easy escape,, and someone wanted to sit next to her and Joy said fine and it was Ron, and said nice too meet you and same here! But Joy told him to sit next to the window and she was near easy exit to get away. then he started to talked with her, but she was a bit distract and didn't wants to talks and said Joy I am a bit tired and I just wants to sleeps, fine and I just wanted to be friendly, well you are probably a new Yorker, so how you are tying to insult me? No but that is true about New Yorker, thanks a lot, I really didn't wants to hears right now, when I am heading home, so am I but I live in Connecticut, well that is nice and why did you end up in Texas, well they said it was a safe zone, oh I sees and what was your purpose, the same.

Then Joy fell asleep and Ron looked out of the window and was staring out and then he though he saw a comet was coming out of the sky and he couldn't believe what was happening but he didn't wake up Joy and didn't alert anyone on the train and was silent all the ways home, and then there were sound and boom and everyone was sleeping but Ron was not and he was ready for anything that would happen, Ron was looking out the window and so far he didn't sees anything at that moment he got up and pull the stop for train and then the train stop at this point and Ron pointed out there were about three bodies on the track and one of them was moving and now what? So they sat in the train and then they saw soldiers coming in and removing the bodies and about ten minutes the train was moving and Joy said you spotted that and I am surprise about the military being there so quick , I guess they have too gets rid of the dead body and not to have the epidemic again, that true, hope that we get home much quicker and Ron said on rails I bet we will sees mores of dead bodies, you don't says! Well it is true, and we cannot catch what they had, then the epidemic would start again! about one minute later they were getting closer and the train stop and what going on and I don't but I hope there are no- more zombies here!

The train stop for about one hour delay and Ron and Joy were a bit jumping and not patience and they asked the conductor when they were leaving and he shook his head and said I don't know, well are we okay? What do you means? Well we are in danger but we are been told not to move at this time of elimination zombies and then we can move and now we are waiting for the order from the united states to go on, well I guess there are a few zombies around and they why we have too stay here for our own protection and obey the law, of the government, well your right but I am still wanted to be home and with my family and about ten minutes that Joy spoke, the solider storms in and said everyone need to get off the train immediately, and Ron is asking how comes? I cannot answer that question just obey my orders and you will be fine. Okay we will and when they got off the train, they carried on the corpses on the train and Joy said I don't like this, I don't neither but we have no choice, and then everyone back all board on the train, and Joy said I cannot go on that train you must don't be so suspicious and they will locked you up,, thanks! Late that night, Ron got up and looked around and when inside that morgue that they set up in the train and make sure that no one would sees him and then Ron came back and told Joy that they situation is in order and the corpses are dead and they will not come back to lives, and how do you know I don't!

But we will be fine and we are headed home and our family are waiting for us and try to think positive and I am but I just wander where my friend when? Oh you means Tom well he is secret services and he is at the border and searching for mores zombies infection well if he told you that he was just a guy to save you that is totally bullshit, well he is the one that check out the virus and if you were infection you were be in shoot and in flames and dead, thanks for that warning well he is gone and I have nothing to worry about so, I am heading home anyway, that is true!

Going Home

Joy and Ron got really close and but one thing that he said don't get attach too me, but why I just wants to be close and we are going to different direction so, and that is true, yes I know but you are like a loner not really and I lost a lot persons in this epidemic and so I don't want to be near anyone at this point and I don't what tomorrow will bring, well that true but do you know something that I don't? so are you asking me a question what going on? Well it seem it is not over but it is being quiet from the public and then what you are saying it is not over but why are we on the train, maybe it is a distract and so we don't find out anything well you are scaring me at this point I just wants to jump out of the train well they probably shoot you, I don't like that scenario just sit and don't paid any attention on us, do you understand? Yes! Then Ron fell asleep and then Joy and then they started to hears moaning and groaning and banged in trying to break in and then Ron suddenly got up and then saw the conductor standing with his hand was off and then it was dripping off blood and said wanted to wake up Joy, but she was sleeping deep and but Ron was afraid that he were get bitten and he pull out the spray to him and then Joy got up, said he is a zombie, and she knock him down and where are the rest of the peoples I don't know, Joy I think we having a problem I don't wants to hears that but we need to jump off the train are you crazy? No but what other choice do we have? Well we can stay on the train and there is one zombie, I think,, well there might be mores. I am worry and where are the zombies and then Joy peek through the hole and said there are more than one, no we are trapped, why did they put the zombies on the train, I don't know and then she notice that Tom was standing guard and then she called out too him and he pushed the door and said don't

136

comes close and put some chains and locked it and Joy said you cannot stayed there! I must be here! But why? I was infection and that why I am locked up for my own good, but you are not dead and they can take you to the hospital but it is too late, in my blood stream and I will died and then become a zombie., no I don't believe you. That is true, just go back in case the door crack open you jump out of the train. But Joy was begged him to join them and I said I cannot and you protection yourself and others if you have too. About one hour they heard sirens going off and now we are in trouble but why because of the sirens and the epidemic strike again!!! ands we are trapped and so what did your friend says we need to get off on the next stop, but won't we run into zombies probably we were but we should gone to the "west coast" you are right but now it is too late, yes but let jump off soon, hope that we will be able too and then they started to says " we wants brains" we do have problem and you are right! But let go and jump but the train is moving too fast and then it was taking a short curve and almost crash into the pole and now we need to go at this moment, when Joy said started too spoke suddenly the train stop, and now what? The door open wide and they were coming and now what? Well the zombies are coming no kidding! They will grab us and killed us, quiet, they do smelled us., that is the true, well shut up and the first zombie step in was Tom and he was drooling and trying to grab my arms and I was fighting him off and now I just jump off and the solider were shooting at me and I thought at that moment I were gets shot and I just duck down and miss by a inch and I was still not safe, and I ran into the woods and I hid and then Ron followed me and I we were both safe and then the solider came with sniffing dogs to follow our trail and now I told Ron we needed to go into the water and the scent were be smelled and that is a good idea and then we stay in the lake and hid in the bushes and I notice the house on the lake and we will go there! that is a good plan.

Yes it is and let go but need to make sure it is clear!

Old creepy house

Joy said to Ron I sees a house and it looked beautiful so do we go there? yes we should there, okay I will follows you and we will be fine don't let the soldiers sees us I won't! No one is behind us and we are fine right now that is good and the house looked like a mansion, yes it does and I think we can stay overnight and then we can stay there for awhile, yes and I hope that have food in the house, and they approach the house and suddenly the door was wide opens and Joy said well it must be a good signs, I guess so.

They both steps inside and then the door shut and Joy said did you close the door and Ron said I didn't I thought you did? No, well I don't like this right now, seem like we are not alone in this house, what do you mean? Well I think that we are in the house of ghosts. What I feel that eerie sound and cold with the chill and I don't like this and then Joy tried to open the door and it were not opened, now what? Then Joy saw shadows in the dark and Ron said, I think that we are in a haunted house, you must be kidding and then Ron said I sees a cemetery in the back of the yard, well this house is a mansion but not among the living but the dead, so we have zombies somewhere out there and now we are trapped in this house with ghosts, so I don't understand? Well we thought this house was an ordinary house and now we are still here! Then the lights flicker and the table move and glass falling off the counter and chairs in different direction, and I don't wants to stay here and then they got into the library and Joy said that we need to gets out of the window now, and she pick up the chair and threw it out of the window and it didn't even crack and then Joy and Ron saw a little girl standing in the library and I went up to her and I asked where is your mom and dad and then she started to cried and then Joy said, I believe we need to run now and I don't know if we will be able to get out, and I am not staying here and end up like the peoples in this haunted house, we will find a way out, sure, yes I am. Ron said maybe we should go through the basement and then we can go out the from the cellar and open the hatch and walks upstairs out, it sound a good idea, but we are being watched, I know but watched your steps, I am and then they reach the hatch and it were not open and about a moment later, Joy, and then Ron lost his balance and at that moment I couldn't catch him and he slam on the floor and hit his head and lay there and I ran too him and he had his eyes close and I tried too wake him up and then he said I am fine and are you sure? Yes I am but seems like he was all right and when he got up, he saw his body and then Joy said you are dead the house took you, no I am not! Then Ron looked and said you are right! Later that night Joy said I cannot go out there alone and I wants you comes with me, I cannot I am trapped in this house and it will not let you go! Now do you know that's I just do!

I will get out, go I will try to help you, so Joy ran but forgot to says goodbye to Ron and then the hatch close and then smoke and Joy couldn't sees where Joy was going and then Joy got dizzy and fell down and lay there for few hours and now she became a ghost of that house and alls the ghosts said welcome to home., Joy, no I don't wants to be there and I am not dead, then Ron said why did you comes back here? I wanted to says bye too you and then I was smoother with smoke and I didn't know where I was going and I collapse and now I am here, well it was stupid for you to comes back and says bye and you know that I was dead and now we live in this creepy willow house on the lakes that when you enter you don't escape, well that is too late, so it is my fault I notice that house from the train station and now we are trapped here forever and we will roam the house and we will never be alive again! Joy said to Ron and no one will find us and we will have our bodies never find here, that is true and we will never be in the grave and we will be living in this haunted house, sorry about that's'!

Dark Shadows in the old creepy house

It was on the night of Halloween and they pass there the woods to Katy house and then Joanne and Jeff stops in the front of the house and said did you sees that's ? what I am not sure, well I thought I saw like shadows inside that house, you must be kidding and I am not and then Jeff did you sees that's? no I have not, what you trying to scare me, I think that you are going a good job, and don't scare me again, promise, okay scary cat I won't and they kept on walking and then Jeff said why don't we just looked inside, you must be crazy and I am not going inside, well I am you can wait for me outside, okay I am coming but we will be late for the party, it will just takes five minutes and then we will go to Stacy house and maybe coming back we can just go back inside and looked around the room and maybe we can find some treasures, well I just want to be at Stacy and you took me here on the detour and now I am not sure which ways to go, comes on Joanne, and Jeff inside and then Jeff felt the draft and then a chill and then eerie sound and creaking sound and some footsteps walking toward them and Jeff tried to push Joanne out but she fell and hit her head and it bleed and Jeff apologize and I am sorry I bought you here and we will go now, and he pick her up and her out and then Joanne woke up and said what happened to me, you will be fine, I sees them, but who do you sees, I sees the dead, oh you cannot sees them. Your not a child unless your dead, no I am alive and I don't even have a headache and I am just want to get to the party, fine, let go now, and Joanne and Jeff walks for a mile and Joanne said I need to rest for a while., and then Jeff saws three zombies on there trail and it is not good and I think we took the wrong turns, please don't says that they are very quick and I just don't wants to be lost in the woods right now so keep on walking and we will get to Stacy house, so how far and I am a bit tired right now and I need to rest after getting the bump on my head. It was my fault and we will stay here for awhile.

About half hour later they reach Stacy house and the lights were off and Joanne said what going on are late, are we in the wrong location? Why are you asking we are not lost and we are at the right address, so let step inside and one thing that they didn't know the house disguise and it was the haunted house and not Stacy house and then Jeff said it seems like we have been here before and Joanne said you are right! Looks at the furniture,, I am this is the house that I fell and hurt my head and it somehow got us back, Jeff said I don't believe you, looks Jeff don't sees that fireplace and no friend Stacy, definite you are right so how do we escape I don't know but we cannot stayed here so go out Joanne,, and I am but it not letting me out and if we do go out the zombies will grabbed us, so we have no choice but now you are listening to the "Ghosts" and now we can be trap here and but if we do go out they will get us and have our brains, well I don't wants to end up dead neither ways, that is true, we need to make the right choice and then we can get back home and then Joanne said we are home all ready, stop saying that Joanne., well I am going to try to escape and follow that path that we can into this place, and walks through the cemetery and then we can go home and miss the party. Well if we didn't go to the detour we probably were have some pizza and some beers and now we are struck and no ways out and now you are blaming me,. Yes you were the one that wanted to shown me this mansion and now this home will be forever but we are not dead yet! But we also cannot get out and then she heard Joy and said I will help you out and I am trapped here and I will open the door and you will be able to go and then Tom said you cannot let them go it is there destiny, no she was trick to be here and we should let her home and the Jeff will stay here,, no the rule is that they both stayed, go Joanne I will freed you, thanks!

Destination

At this moment Joanne and Jeff to escape and then Joy called out and said runs out and don't let the others ghosts catch you and then Tom slam the door and once again, then Joanne and Jeff fell into the basement and they were surround by Ghosts and then they said "welcome" to your new home and then Joanne said I hope that I wake up and it was only a nightmare, well missy it is not and you are trapped forever, and I wants to go home and we cannot release you because you are one of us and welcome and I just don't like it, well you should have never steps inside this house and Jeff never told you were you were end yours destination and so I have nothing else too says but just don't get into our ways and we will get along and thanks Jeff, this is how I will be spending Halloween, and not returning home that really bug the hell out of me and because of you, so you will be bitching about this and I didn't force you too go inside but you just when inside to looked around and don't blame me, but you bought me here and I didn't know my ways home so now I am in this haunted house., and about a minute later, a few zombies came inside and then Joanne said they will get us but they won't because your not a live, thank for the reminder, that I am dead and then zombies the words saying "Brains" and we are ghosts and we have nothing to worry about like a ten minutes later,, Stacy and Steve came to the house and I tried to warns them that zombies in the house and but I couldn't touch her and then Stacy saw them coming and then Steve pull her away and then shut the door, said I wander if Jeff and Joanne are I hope they are on there ways, well we have to deal with these zombies and I don't have any weapon and we might end up being dead meat, that true, but I am going to beat them and I am not going to let them get me, sure they are behind us and we have no place to hide and then Joanne somehow open the door and Stacy and Steve ran out and more zombies are coming toward us and I don't know if we should go back into the house, no we should go to the car and drive away and I will knock down a few, great plan, yes it is and I am not going to argue with you and I am just going to be in back of you and then the front door shut and then they ran for there live ran to the car and stop and Stacy and Steve said I drop the keys in the house and I need to get them, otherwise we will be stuck here and that is not our destination, I do hears you and don't be long and I will try to held off the zombies and that way you can get back inside. Can you start the car without those key, you must be kidding, no I am not I am totally serious and I just wants to leaves this terrible place and I agree and I do wants to get back home and hope that my family are fine and not invaded by zombies and I just left the house open and they can just step inside and eat them up and don't says that, but hurried get those keys and I will be fine, good and I will locked the door and I will wait until you comes back and then Stacy and Steve and Steve walks back and Stacy was waiting and like biting her nail and terrify and wait and wait and no sign of Steve and then they looked out and it was her friend Joanne and standing near the car and said go away they wants you and it is the house that wants you and Steve, get out of the car and run into the woods, well I will get caught by zombies, no you won't you are scaring me and I just wants to be left alone, and the clock strike midnight and Joanne said I have warns you and your friend will not comes back, you are lying no I am not! I was your friend and you know that I were not lies, but you are a ghost, I know but you out here you will be zombies dead meat, then she saw Steve coming toward the car and barely making it toward her and then fell down to the ground and there were zombies ready to eat him up and then Stacy got out of the car and ran up to them and knock them down and pull him away and but he was bitten and then Stacy cried out and said why him?

Alone in the woods, went back to the house

Stacy took the keys and got into the car and it were not start at first and then it and Stacy was driving away and with a lot of tears in her eyes. Screaming and yelling and saying why did I tells him to take me to that house and now I don't know how to get home and I think that I am lost, and Stacy drove for hours and hours and then stops and saw that house and didn't realized that house was the place that she loss Steve and it was so beautiful and inviting and so Stacy decided to park the car in the end of the fence and walks toward the door and the door open up and Stacy was like a trace and like she was home, and step inside and she was surrounded and but she didn't sees Steve and then she saw Joy and Tom said what are you doing here? I told you too go home but you stupid bitch you are back and so welcome to your home, what? I am not staying if you continue you will be living here and you will be trapped forever and I think you don't wants to died, but out there are zombies and this the only place that I can hide for awhile, no gets out of here now, yes keeps going on, I will and you need to hide in the woods and wait until daylight and walks to the main road and walks, I am warning you, I know you are and just go! Stacy was a bit frighten and scare and alone and but Stacy walks out and didn't looked back and then walks and saw the Zombies and hid in the bushes and then when it was clear and kept on walking and reach the train station and got on the train and saw it was okay but didn't notice that they were dead.

Stacy sat down and didn't pays a attention and the train started to move and one of the character said I wants to drink your blood and he had fang and Stacy thought herself it must be a Halloween costume, but he was not in costume and now Stacy wanted to get off but she couldn't have a way of distract the passenger so Stacy sat quiet and didn't make a move than the train stop and Stacy jump off and ran into the woods. And was relief .

Moon Eclipse, Days of Darkness

Vampires! Human Bloods

Daylight

Stacy realize that she was almost venous by Vampires and before that in a haunted house, and also ran into zombies, and it was a bad day around and now on the train with Vampires and that was a close called and didn't like the scenario and just wanted to be with the living and not the living of the dead and that day I headed to the diner to get some food and it seems like it was okay and at this point I am sure where I was at this time but I knew for now I was safe. I walks in and I sat at the table and the waitress took my order and I just sat there and then my food came and I was wander if I was close home and if I should asked her but I didn't want but any suspicious on myself so I was quiet and ate my foods and I asked if I could have carrot cake and then some coffee and the waitress Beth said well you must be new here? I never seen you before and I asked her, and she told me that I was in New York State., the border of Canada and I told her about the train ride and she warns me not too take the train at night, and I nodded my head and I said okay but I do need a place to stay overnight until I get back home and Beth also warn me to be inside by dust, and then I said the creature of the night? Beth nodded her head and said yes, but don't trust anyone that you don't know include me, but why? This place has a vampires what? I don't understand? I have warns you, I need to do my job and if you don't feel about hotel you can stay with me, okay! I am just rest talking too you and I feel good vibes from you, once again I could be the evil one don't says that, can stay with you one night and then I will find the ways home, fine with me and then after she ate, Beth told her where she lives and gave her the key and told her not too let anyone but her inside her place, I will and don't worry I won't invite a vampires, good, and I do have some holy water and cross that will protection you, thanks for your help.

Then Stacy walks out and walked few blocked and got to Beth apartment.

Stacy unlock the door and make sure it was opens and then shut it tight and about 8pm, Stacy heard sound like moaning and groaning and banged and booms and then she saw the building burning. What will do and I don't sees Beth and hope that she is okay? But Stacy walks out but then changed her mind and when back inside and then someone wanted to grab her legs and said I am not going out here, and before she closed the door she saw bats flying around and zombies walking the street, it was the night of the dead, and now Stacy was really terrify and when into the living room and sat there and waited and waited for Beth too come home but she didn't shown up that night but she called and said I am stuck in the diner and I will not be coming tonight and I said what going on? Now I cannot explains too you but I will later and Stacy hung up on her and the phone was dead. About ten minute later, Stacy looked out of the window and saw them walking and bat bitten the innocence and at that moment a bat came to the window and knock and said let me in, and I just turned around and closed my eyes and pray that I were not be next and then the rain came and wind and the thunder and lighting and now I was really terrify, and the lights when out and now I had a candle and I lit it and I just cuddle into a blanket and somehow I feel asleep and the next morning the sun was out and I knew that I couldn't stay another night so I when to the diner but seems like it was old and with cobweb and I just left the key on the table that I had dinner and I left the note and I just kept going and didn't stop and turned around and I just thought I was in a bad nightmare and I wanted to gets back home that day. Went I got to the train station and alls the train were leaving at midnight and I said no ways, if I have too I will walks home, so I went to the highway and then I saw a car and I looked around and I just sat inside and I started up in the red mustang and drove away, at this point I didn't sees the dead corpse in the bed seat and then I just stop!

Heading home with a dead body

No, I need to get rid of that body and I need to get home and I am not sure if I am taking the right highway home. But I am willing to take the old highway and get the hell out here, but I don't know if that body will wake up and bite me and I don't know if I am going to be a zombie or vampire at this point but I make sure that I rid of body and buried it in the ground and then, and I can just head home and then I saw that tall handsome man standing on the side of the road and at that moment I didn't know if I pick him up and but then he is stranger and I am alone and I do have a dead body in the car, so I will just keeping going and then I think if I don't pick him up and he might just gets killed by vampires and the zombies roaming the street and then I think, then I decided yes I will and I will cover the body with the sheet and then I will give him a lift but I have to make sure that he is not a vampire and how do I do that's, and I thought and then I stop and said do you wants a ride and he nodded his head, yes I would to the town and that ways they can get the tow truck and then I can wait until they fix the car, so what happen and I am not sure exactly but I am glad that you came by and pick me up, I was afraid that some creature would have me has a meal, I don't understand. He steps inside and sat and turned around and said what is that's don't be so nosy and well no it is my stuff and don't touch and all right! Then he just sat and looked at me like a was a criminal and but I was not and then he said I smell something, do you have a body and it is dead and did you killed that person? No I have not and then Stacy was afraid that he were squeal to the police about the body in my car but I just realize that police might be vampires and zombies too.

But I still was quiet when we got to the town and I stop and he step out at the gas station talks with the man and told him about his car and I just left in a hurried and I drove away and didn't looks back at day!

Later that day I dump the body into a hole in the woods and buried it very deep and then I heard like wolf like they were howling and I ran to the car and drop the shovel and got to the car and drove away and got to the town and check into the hotel and ran into the hot guy and we talked and we had dinner and then he came to my room and he said I don't like this town it is kind of creepy and spooky and I don't understand. Looks well I am what wrong? Well looks how they are dressed, maybe how there boss wants them to wear, just an uniform and do you think so, yes and then well my name is Larry and I am an Stacy and I am from the east coast and I think that eight days storm that lasted for the eight days and everything happened and peoples that died and they turned into zombies and then the vampires came later and I don't know how that happened but I did go into a creepy house and they were ghosts that wanted to me to stay and I refuse and but my friend got trapped in the house, I don't know if I believe what you are saying but it sound crazy, and then Larry looked out, there are zombies and vampires in the street and how do we escape, remember I have my car parked in the back, are you nuts in the alley, where they prey on you and I am not stepping out from here, if you don't you will died, no I will not, comes with me now about ours foods., well we will go some place and about my car don't worry about it, you can use my car, well your car is not a classic like mind, okay do you wants to lives? I do wants to live and I am going with you and hope that we find a good safe location and then the waitress said your foods is ready and you are trying to stiff me., no we take it and pays on the ways out and waitress said well you better stay inside, you will end up dead if you go outside, you will end up dead, I don't wants to hears you.

We are still going and well you are risking your life and Beth the waitress said stay here, and I will make sure that I will keep you safe, and then they saw her fangs. No, I am a vampire and I do not drink human blood.

Midnight

Stacy and Larry said we are in a town trapped by vampires, and the zombies roamed the streets and they are hungry for bloods and brains and I don't wants to the meal for neither species, I don't neither but how do escape from here, I don't know but I am not going to walks the night like a dead, I refuse, so do I and it is my fault and I stop and drove here and I thought it was a safe town but it is far, far from the city, I know but now we need a plan,, one of us need to distract them and I have the car keys and I will get the car and then I will drive up the diner and then you run out and then we will leaves this town, well it is getting dark and I know but I think it will works,, and then Stacy said, I am feeling weak, and what did our waitress gave us, I don't know, and she looked at Larry, your face looked old, I don't know what you are saying? Are you a zombies? I don't know how to answers and so maybe I am, well but at first I seen you, you were alive, yes I was and then when you left me behind something happened to me and how I am the creature of the night, no I will not accept that, you must and I will help you to gets out, I promise I won't hurt you, but can I have a taste of your blood, no you cannot, they wants to feast on you, I won't let them, do you hears that's ! but I don't if they going to listen what you are saying, and I will let you out, fine, I need to get away, now silent they hears you and I don't wants that for you because helped me out when I was stranded in the woods and you save me and now it is my turned. Thanks and I will tried to help you but you cannot, I am dead and I feed on blood and you need there is no saving me but I need to save you, and the waitress said don't you help this girl out of here, and anyway that you helped her, we will drain alls your blood, do you understand, yes master, I do, and he wink at Stacy and run for your life and

I will helped you, I know I should not turned you because you betray us, and you will died, please don't do it, I will not let her go! Stacy I am sorry I need to do it, and you will become one of us, and I could drain alls your blood, but I won't but I will make you vampire, no please let me go, there is more vicious vampire that will break you into pieces and I think you were rather I just bite and you turned into one of us, would like that's no I just wants to go back to my family and if I was bitten I probably were bite them and killed them, I think your right! But still I need to bite you, please no,, don't do it too me, remember that I helped you but I cannot because I am not the same man that I was, well think the night on that dark road and I gave you that ride but you took me to vampire hell and now I am one of them,, I am sorry that I had to get rid that corpse and left you here, but I did comes back for you but you came too late, so leave and he hit the waitress and Stacy ran out of the diner and went into the car and got inside and I put the key inside and the steer wheel and it was locked and then I tried again and then I just dash out and then I saw those zombies walking toward me and I turned right and then left into main stretch of highway and I was headed out from there and I just keeps on driving and the road were pitch black and I couldn't sees where I was going at that moment, and then I just stops for a moment and I saw a sign and I was headed east and then west of that highway, and now I was not stress out and I was more relax and then I was on my guard. Once again I need to stop and I when to the gas station to pick up some water and then at that moment I just passed out and about two hours later,. I saw Larry and Beth and said I thought I left, no you had a bad dream and then you were just feeling faint and then I caught you and carry you on the bed and then I thought I drove out and I was at the gas station, well you thought about it and but you never left but was at the gas station, no you were dreaming, that not in possible, but that what happened, so I will shown you that your car is parked where you left it with me, and your not a vampire? Nope!

Terror in the street

D
o you sees what going on here? Yes and I think that we need to get
to the hotel and but I am not sure how that going to happened,
that a good question, yes it is Larry and I am really scare and I
thought you were a vampire and so was Beth, well you just ate something
that didn't agree with you, oh I sees, what was it? well it was a vegetable that
prevent that zombies and vampires would go after, so it is urban legend, I
think it is and I think we will be fine, well I don't that they could break in
and eat us up and that is not good, I know but we have no choice and don't
attempt to step out, don't you sees the terror in the street? I do and I don't
wants them coming in here, so listen to what I am saying, I will, but be
silent and don't let them hear you, but you are walking toward the window
and they sees you and you are showing that they have fresh meat, well I
think you crazy and paranoid and if you feel that ways, why don't you just
leave, and then Stacy I don't want to get massacre, you will they catch you
and eats your guts and brains and body parts, that is I don't wants to hears,
so just take the sit and I will called the sheriff and he will comes and gets
us, do you think that he will make it through that crowds? Yes I do and
he will be wearing something that smell like the dead, maybe he is one of
them, and about a minute later, they heard someone saying help me, help
me and I looked and no one was there, and I have a bad feeling that they
will come in and get us so we need to go up to the attic and Stacy asked
do you trust her? Why we might be bait.

Why are you saying that we are bait? We are don't let her kid you, and
but you do trust me? Yes of course but we are in some kind of trapped
and I cannot explains it, and about one hour later, Stacy and Larry and
Beth hid in the attic and her boss was looking for her and then he make a

mistake of letting the dead inside and he screams and yells and said help me, they are eating me up and they are drinking alls my blood and then he fell down.

Heard her head and then got up and said what happen to me and they didn't answers her but looked around again and I am fine and I am with friend and soon we will be leaving this awful place, and I am not staying here alone, do you hears me, yes I do but there are vampires outside and they will eat us up! No, they will not gets us, but the y are on the hunts, I sees that's!

Vampires were prowling inside the diner and searching for the survive and Stacy was very frighten and Stacy said what happen to your boss, well he is torn into pieces and he is dead like a door nail, well do hears me clear, loud and clear, well we have a bad situation to deal with and we have no ways out of this attic, but only the front door that was open by my boss and he let them in and now they are searching to drink our blood, I am really scare and terrify and do you have some holy water and crucifix in this place, no I don't we need to make stake and killed them, they are powerful and they will get you, no I am not going to died because of a vampire, and a zombies, well I don't what to says but we need to stick together until morning and then think a way out, good idea and who will do watched and Larry said I will.

Later that night, Larry was watching the attic door but he just got a bit tired and doze for a minute and then Stacy heard a creak the door and woke up quickly and shut it tight, and started to yelled at Larry and said you fell asleep and they were almost in, you wants us to be dead? Of course not and now Beth was acting a bit nutty and Stacy said why is she acting this ways I don't have a clue, it must be this place, well I don't want to be here but we need to stay until morning, do you understand? Yes otherwise they will gets us, promise that you will save me., I will! Take my word, I will and then time when by and it was quiet and then it started it again and I don't like this and we have to stay put, okay but you know that I am not patience, well in this case you need too, fine but I don't like it not at alls, and then Larry said looks my cell is working and I can called someone for helped good and tell them where we are and then they can come and find us.

Stacy was being silent and then he gave her a kiss and then she when back to sleep and dreamt that she was home and everything was fine but when she woke up and she saw that she was alone and called out and no one answers. Looks they are in the windows and they are going to get inside because someone invite them and we will be massacre and killed. Run, and run found a crucifix and we need to found some stake to killed those vampires now and looked around if there are any holy water and about the zombies, well I don't sees any weapons and but we need to hit there brains and then they will died but first we need to killed the vampires. But don't looked into the vampire eyes and they will make you do things and they will drain your blood, so how do you know the history of vampires, well I read and watched a lot of horror flick and that how I know but this is real lives and I know but we need to not to be seen, and they must not get into the attic, got it! but Stacy took off her gold cross and shine it through the window and one of the vampire fell to the ground and then some ugly vampire just broke the window and tried to get inside and I just pull down the window and then I put the cross on his face and he started to burned, and fell and there more than 10 and they didn't enter, but then Beth looked into his eyes and fell for his spell and then she was in a trace and then she invite him inside and then he suck her blood and she fell to the floor and about ten minute she became a vampire and wanted to bite Stacy and Larry and they jump out of the window when the sunlight came in and the rest of the vampires turned into dust and Larry and Stacy ran into the car and drove away from quickly and they were safe so far and they drove and drove and until they reach New York city that day and they didn't wants to think what happen that day, and Larry and Stacy didn't say anything to anyone that day.

Night of the comet

When they arrives to the city and tonight will be a sighting of the comet,, and Stacy said to Larry I am not going to stand outside and watched the comet so I will go to bed and don't think what happened last night and did it really happen? Of course I did and it was not a nightmare, no but it really,, fine but wake me up in the morning I will and I will take a shower, fine but don't use too much of the hot water. Did you sees those persons standing out there and watching the sky for that comet too comes down and I know that is ridicules and I think I just take a shower and you can watched on the TV and that is a good idea, I agree and so Stacy when into the shower about twenty minutes later, the a big flashing light came through and I called out to Larry did you sees that's ? yes I did and I looked out of the bathroom window and I just saw clothing on the ground and I thought what happened to those peoples, and then I came out of the shower and Larry was fast asleep and I decided to gets dressed and check outside but I though I should wake up Larry and not to go alone and then about ten minutes later I saw zombies coming from around alls corners and now I needed to wake up Larry and tells him what going on and I think he will called me crazy but I am not but I looked again and the clothes still on the streets and sidewalks and what really happened to them and now I am very worried and I thought to myself are we going to died and is there poisonous in the air and did they vanish and turn into dust, that is terrible, that is true but I don't wants to be static but I do wants to live to we need a face mask? That I was thinking when we step out will be vaporize? Then I thought well I am not steeping outside until they says so and then Larry woke up and said I think it time to go, no I am going until it is clear, fine, your not leaving me alone, well I am not staying, but it is dangerous out there and there are a lot of zombies, you are crazy, no I am not, it happen when the comet came down and it change the world again, I don't know but I don't like it, but we cannot stay here neither, and we have to no choice we need to leaves this place, it the comet cause that affect we need to leave immediately and go where? Just keeps driving and get away from the polluted air from here and cover your face, no kidding I will and you do the same, and about the vampires, they could be instinct, are you saying that vampires are in the dust, yes and now we need to deal the after affect of the comet and find a place where the air is clear. But seems like it polluted the whole population and we are in the middle of the air and the zombies and they wanted our brains and some could be our friends and we cannot even helped them out and we are just stuck with the undead but we are still alive but for how long I don't know but let go and run to the car and started up and then we can go further south and head to Mexico, do think that is a good location and I think that we have no choice but Mexico, I don't like that.

But we need to move right now without any hesitates and just walks out and then try not to get bite and then get into the car and drive and I don't like this and I don't like it neither but this is our life now we could be alone in the world and we need to survive this someday everything will be okay again! that is true, said Stacy to Larry and I think your definite right and I am ready to go and make sure that you hit them on the head, make sure that you don't get any drool on you that can be the virus, you are right and it is don't get bitten and don't get drool on your face and I know, just follow me, okay I am in back of you and don't you sees that girl, not exactly, now do you sees her, nope, looked straight ahead and okay now I sees her, should we helped her, well yes, but she could be a zombie, but the other case she might be okay, well we are going to stop and pick her up and then we will take her to Mexico and do think that she will trust us, I don't know but I think we should tried, and they drove up too her and stop and they looks!

Lost Girl

No we need to drove away quickly what wrong with her she is a zombie and she wanted to gets inside and no your seeing things, what do you means your mind is playing trick on you, I think that she is vampire, looked at her fanged, and she looked like a zombie, but they dash away and now the lost girl following with a fast speed and she was so near the car and somehow she got in front of the car and stop with her hands and stop the car and at that moment the car skid in the ditch and into the mud and I tried to get out but now we are stuck and then the "Lost Girl" came up to the window and smash the window and tried to drag me out and Larry and we tried to defeat her but it were not occurs and right now I felt a panic and I thought it was the last of us but then Larry pull out a stake and tried to put into her and then she got on my side and tried to get me out of the car and now I thought I was doom, but then it seems like stop for a moment and the sun was coming up and somehow she just disappear in the air and didn't sees that lost girl again and I was relief but we still were in danger of those walking dead were approaching us and I said we cannot drive, so we had gets out the car and run for our life and I couldn't believe what was going on and those zombies would saying we wants your brains and Larry said you cannot have it, but Larry they don't understand what you saying and I think we really got run like you never did before, got it. later that night they got to a campsite and Larry said we will hide out here and that is a good idea until we find a other car and drive to Mexico, I still says that is danger zone with vampires, don't says that I think your wrong I hope that your right! But silent they hears us and I don't wants them to smell us and we need to get our self wet and they scent will be gone, so I don't sees any water around here and I think the shower is broken here and we don't have anything to protection us here and we will be dooms, stop it, I will cover my ears if you saying again!

About two hours later, the lost girl was staring at us, and watching our move and she also got the zombies to comes this ways and now I was really terrify and I think that we were in Zombies area and I think that they will be trying to break inside and we will end up dead, neither torn into pieces and the other scenario is that ours bloods suck out of life, that is a terrible feeling, well we are like sitting ducks and now we need to get the hell out of here, do you hears me., definite I do and now what? One of us we need to distract them, and it will not be me, said Stacy and I really cannot run fast and they probably were chew me up and spite me out and I don't like this.

I don't like it but we need to face reality right now, and it seem like we are not going to make it and I think we should prepare for the worst and I don't like you repeating the worst scenario and we should have some fate and hope that we will make it through the night and I like your positive thinking and surviving this and then we can walks out of these wood and head to safe haven and not in zombies world and that really suck and because that little lost girl was a vampire, and she cause this chaos and if I sees her I am going to stake her and she will turned into dust and then we will fight those zombies and get the hell out of here, I promise on my life, I do believe what you saying and I hope that we make it through but I do wants to make love too, just in case that we don't make it, well I don't like what yours saying now, I refuse to used you in the passion of love and I believe making love with the one that you loved and not just anyone do you know what I am saying and so you saving yourself for the one you love and it is possible, that were happened, yes, fine, just seems like you don't like me and don't want me to be close too you, and I don't need this you being a bitch and I am trying my best for us to make it alive, okay sorry about such a bitch with you and I just want to be home in a room with heat and water and being with friends and I am not asking too much, am I?

Darkest Hours

No, you are not but I think that we are not alone, no you told me that zombies were out there, well also vampires, you must be kidding, and we are surrounded by them, no I don't wants to listen to that I am too depressant about this and I wants to cried and remember don't invite a vampire and where is your cross and I don't know I probably lost it in the woods I don't know about the crucifix and I have no clue in the car, I guess. But what are we doing to do, said Stacy and Larry but we will figure out and we will not gets bitten by the darkness of those creature of the night that sucks blood and feed on human, and I just don't wants to be in the middle of that's it is bad enough with the zombies and now we have to deal with the vampires that really sucks, well I wants to gets some holy waters and some gun and bullets to blast that those zombies to hell, well be don't have the weapons and so we are defeat by them, thanks a lot about having confidence and I just don't want died in some hick town and become a living of the dead, well I guess how life deal a hand and so if this is our fate, so be it. you are such a loser and about you, you are afraid of your own shadow and when you sees the zombies coming you crawl on the floor, well I don't want them to break in just like the vampires and someway the zombies gave the vampire to come in without being invited and I think it only you and me and those thousand and us and we have no chance of defeat, stop being such a baby and fight like a man and not a coward, well missy you don't helped me out and you hide in the corner and there was a time that one of the zombie almost got me and you then came to rescue me and then I save your ass, and you don't even thanks me, okay I am thanking that you save my fucking ass so many times and I do appreciate it and but sometime you are acting like a jerk, and so let work together and then we can beat the hell of out of those zombies and vampire and we will be freed to walks and not be scare to death,, got it Larry and loud and clear, and the sun is going down and now it going to be more dark than light and now what are we going to do? Be silent and tried not make get a attention and tried not make sound, got it and you do the same, and then the lights when out and candles were getting lower and lower and then it was pitch dark and Stacy got very close to Larry and said don't let me go and Larry said I won't and we will be okay and then they were a banged and it was the " Zombies trying too get inside and what are we going to do and then Stacy saw a dark shadow in the same room and was about to grab her and Larry sprinkles some holy water on his face and he turned burned and turned into ash and now there were more coming inside and then Larry pull out the stake and stab him into the heart and fell was dust and now the zombies came in and tried to pull Stacy and then she said, help me, help me, the zombie, got and hurried, I don't wants to be dead meat, but hurried and Larry pull out the gun and fires and almost hit Stacy and what the hell are you doing? Are trying to killed me? No but I did save you, and about a inch I were been dead, and they have hungry for brain and wants us for meal, ands I am not going let them, okay, so we need to get out of this house and then Stacy said, it getting lighter and I think that we should escape now ands too the car and yes but the car is out of gas, well I forgot about that's but then they heard a helicopter above the sky and then Larry waves his hands and Stacy said did they sees you? I don't know but hope that they did and we can just fly way and be safe, hope that they are not pirate, you must be kidding we don't have anything to steal that is true but just run to the car and maybe the helicopter won't comes back but it is landed and I think they saw us and so it is too late, so stop running and just wait for them,, is that good idea, right now we have no choice but wait, now you are the dictator and not me, that true but we on your guard and you don't know if they are going to shoot us, that is true.

Pitch Black

B
ut the sun is going in and we are still stranded here and they are coming and we don't have a visual on them and what is the plan I don't know but I think hide in the bushes., well I could get caught by zombies out here and we are not protection, so we are dead and then they saw flashlights flashing in the woods, they saw two peoples walking toward us and then they introduce themselves and said my name is Peter and this is Joan,, and nice meeting you both and we notice you in the wood and you were a bit out of place and then Peter said we should move on before the zombies will be coming here, they are very close and we seen bodies parts and a lot of guts and we also saw them eating the liver and kidney and even the heart and especially the brain.

There faces were with blood splatter and carried bodies parts and it is really ugh, and I don't even wants to think about it at this time but let go we have to walk about mile to the helicopter and then we will fly south of South Carolina, and I think that place is extinct from Zombies, and we can lay low until the epidemic is over and then we can listen to the broadcast and the special report about the zombies, and also heard that some persons were infection by vampires and but mostly about zombies and but the government is be hush, about what happened and I don't know when it going to end but a lot of peoples died, and of the cause of leak of some kind explosion and it spread very quickly on the east coast and no one is saying what happen and then peoples ended up in hospital and they vomit and then they just collapse and died and it was it and then few hours they woke up and started to walks and then they attack and ate brains, that what I heard said Peter to Larry and Stacy and I don't know but I was in New Jersey and at that time I was in the basement and getting few bottle of wine and then the house shook and I fell to the ground, and I got up and I felt a little weak and then I when upstairs and they wanted to attack me and I ran to Joan house but I was surrounded and Joan came out and had a shotgun and shot them in the head and then we took the car and headed to the airport and found the helicopter and then we fly over and we notice the car and then we knew that you were in trouble and landed and then we came too you but we would not sure that if you were zombies but you speaking so we know that you are not and but it getting really dark now and we need to walks to the helicopter and now and do you understand what I am saying, yes I do and we deal with a few of them too and it was really hard to killed them and well I am ready to go and so I just don't know where the safe place but we will be fine in the sky and they cannot reach us that high, and then what? Can we trust you what we are saying, yes of course, but I would like to know more, but not less talking and walking, they could be hiding and be careful don't give them a some attention they will comes after us quick , because they are fast paces and advance zombies that they can run and they can walks quick and they can eat you up and no one were know that your missing,, they are very high IQ don't says, well whatever they are smarter than we are, you must be quickly, I don't believe you but it is true and I did tape a few and I wants to sees it but first let get to safer place, and I am getting very nerve and stress hang out here, I know but Stacy said you are listening to his bullshit. It could be true and I am not going to argue with him, then he might not take us that is true, and Joan started talking with Stacy and where are you from, well Manhattan, well I am on the other side of town, well they called it Bronx, well that not too bad, nope! Quiet I hears a sound in the woods, so far to do have to go not too far., sure and I am very worry that we won't make it don't panic and we will get there, sure, trust me, I will, and then they alls got on and flew away one more times, and they were relief and then Joan and Peter kissed and Stacy and Larry can you do that later, well it better now, later might be too late.

Strict Area (Do Not Enter)

Joan said to Peter, is this the where we should be flying, in a strict area, so are you afraid, yes I am being we can be shot down and then, they heard a sirens going off and then they heard a sound speaker to leave this area and if you don't we will shoot you down, they are not kidding, I know that why I am flying right out but why are they shooting at us, I don't know but you really messed it up this time and we will end up dead because of you, thanks a lot and then she move away from him. What going on Man? I don't know what you are saying but we are not in the strict areas anymore and I am flying south of the border and we will land in ten minute in that little island, where are we exactly I don't know but we will be here for the night and Peter land the helicopter and they got out and they started to walks around and then Joan said I saw the sign and what did it says, " Strict Area. Do not enter, then Joan came up to Peter, are you suicide, and I don't wants to dies here do you understand? Don't worry I just wants to gets out and don't gets caught, by the guard or whoever watching be careful and watched your steps and I will this is not my first time, here! But if you sees anyone coming just hide in the bushes and don't make the sound and then, and I will be back about less than half hour and please don't let them sees you, you worry too much and I know and I will tried to hurried and fly away from here, no, no, I don't believe it, what they are coming run to the copter now and I am back of you, we need you because your pilot, and none of us don't know how to fly, but then Peter stops and said do you know how to knock down a zombie, and I bet your answer is no, but I will shown you, are looking for trouble, and stop acting like a jerk and comes on and then he stop and said I am going to wrestle a zombie, don't do it, why you think that I will get bit, but I won't, stop it and then he walks fast and then one of the zombie jump him and he was screaming for help, and no one heard.

"Rescue Peter from the zombies

About half hour later, and Joan said where is Peter, and I don't know but we should looked for him, well your right,, and he is your boyfriend and I hope that he is all right, he is probably is, but we need to check on him and I am going to take his shotgun in case, and then Stacy said looked we are surrounded and trapped because of Peter, don't blame him, okay but he did bring us here that is true, but now we need him to fly this copter, that is true, well comes on, I am coming, don't walks too fast, tried to catch up too me, fine, okay, don't be a bitch, I am not. I heard that they are really,, really fast and they can catch up to us and I do have a fear about that's don't you, sure I do and I just wants to be here right now, we need to gets out of here, now I know, but you still not moving and I don't understand? I should tell you that Peter is a risk taker and he doesn't think of others, but himself and when he get into trouble just likes now, he wants us to save him but I think that we should before the zombie would bite him that true and he does know how to fly the copter, true and if don't we will died here too, that is not good and I agree, so Stacy and Joan when into the woods and thought of distract to rescue Peter from the zombies but it was not easy because he was trapped and we didn't know how to do version. But what should we do and well I will run and they will follow me and then Peter will w ill be free and but who will save me, we will said Joan to Stacy, can I trust you? Yes, okay I will do it and we will save Peter and we can leave this awful place, I agree and then Joan make a sound and then Stacy started fireworks and then the zombies looked up in the sky and then Joan grab Peter and pull him away and said where is Stacy in the wood and she will be fine, I told her to meet us at the copter, yes I did but why are you standing here, well I am looking for Stacy and then Stacy started too screamed and help me, they are inches away from me, hurried, we will.

About half hour they reach the helicopter and where is Stacy I don't know but we need to find her and need to leaves soon has we find her, this place is swamp with zombies, your serious, yes I am and let go and find Stacy and Stacy said I am here don't you sees me, and then they saw Stacy and then they took her and they alls ran into the copter and about a dozen of zombies were following them and we would terrify and that they were end dead meat and then Peter said this place is called Territory of Zombies, so how do you that know that I just known and well and if we stay we will be dead meat, so let move and stop talking and let go, fine! Later that day they got aboard the copter and then flew away and didn't looked back once again they were follow by the military and they didn't like that situation and Joan said they think that we are the one that creative the zombies but we were in the wrong place when it occurs well I was in a bunker with a friend. Well that how you got into the situation of zombies and so that was not a easy task about killing these zombies some were like relative and it was really hard but you didn't wants to get infection and you had to destroy them and burned them in the fire and that was our dealing with the zombie and it was a awful situation and so I really cannot explains what really happened when it was the blackout and then the zombies came and they came into the house and try to get us but we ran but we find some weapons and then we just when to the airport and find the copter and since flying and rescue persons that they are not infection likes you, totally well now we will have to fly more south like the Bahamas, and the island should be safe but this one was not just a whole bunch of zombies wanted our brains for foods, so it won't happened again, so how sure are you,, not totally positive but really near but so let me focus where I am going and I don't want to end up at the wrong island, well okay! Meanwhile Joan and Stacy exchange makeup and lipstick and then Joan said don't you have a something that I could change, well no, I don't!

Zombies Territory

Meanwhile Peter kept quiet where he was flying but the Girls were busy putting on Makeup and trying to put on new clothes and about two hours later they landed and Peter said we are here, but Joan and Stacy said this place like familiar, well it is and I left my compass and I need to find it in the woods and Joan and Stacy said we are not going out there, why not I need your help. But we are not moving ours butts and we are staying but Joan and Stacy and you will be spotted by the zombies and you are better off with me, I don't know but we are fine here and don't be stubborn and we are not, and they stay in there seat and then they saw the zombies coming toward them and they jump out and ran to Peter, and Peter said I told you that you were better off with me, but how do we get back but first we need to find the compass and then we will be in good shape, okay! Will it take long? No, I don't think so I don't like being here, I don't neither. About two minute later, Peter was in trouble and then I think this time we will not make it., why are you saying that but it is true and looked we are trapped and maybe we can go through the water and then turn right and left and then go back to the helicopter, but I still didn't find it but I just leave it, are you sure even though now we are in some danger and you not going to take time, to search for it, and why didn't you make it a problem were fine and now we are stuck and because your foolish act to land again on this island, well I am sorry and it will not cut it, don't be too means to Peter, well it is his fault and we are not leaving and we gets caught and eaten by them and no one will rescue us, well I will yelled at him and tell him how I feel that he is selfish son of bitch and I wish that I stay in Manhattan, well you were been dead meat, you don't know that's! yes I do, well you were never survive the zombies invaded in

Manhattan, so now you have knowledge, I do and I cannot denied it, so I don't wants to speak with you now,, I am furious with you and I just don't understand that you are a jerk and stop saying that.

Later that night it rain and they looked for cover and they find a cave. And Joan said is this a good idea,, well that we have to hide for now, okay after the rain, and then we can back track to the helicopter and go leave this place. But once again we need to distract the zombies, and run for our life and do you still have the firecracker? Yes I do and that will gets us out of here and about a mile away, Peter spotted the compass and said now we can go back to the copter and then fly away from here and Stacy was a bit relief and said now a little later I think, it will be clear. How do you know I think these zombies are program but the government, you don't says, yes don't you know that the government keeps things from us, and I think so, well they walks into the cave and two zombies jump out and grab Peter and then Joan and then Stacy took a stick and hit them on the head and now, they alls were in trouble and now what fight and get them in the head and Joan just poke the stick into the head and blood pour out and then outside of the cave., they were saying we wants brains,!! I don't like this, I don't neither and about ten minutes they left the cave and headed to the helicopter and then they were safe and Joan and Stacy jump in the helicopter and then Peter and one of the zombie grab him and pull him out at that moment and Joan jump out and started the fireworks and pull out the gun and shot the zombie in the head and now about ten of the zombies were approaching and now Peter started up the helicopter and we were in the sky and we saw hundred and thousand of zombies on the ground and now I knew that we were safe and Peter flow and said we are going Pennsylvania, but why, I need to check up on a friend and I think that she is okay! But don't but us in a situation of being getting caught by zombies and I won't I promise.

About five hours later they were near and Joan said we are here? Yes!

Mores Flashing Lights

Looks what going on it is happened again! It never stops what? Do you sees what falling from the sky are satellite falling will they make damage the building, no it falling into the water, and it will hit the land, and will start fires, no it will not hit us, no but close. Are you sure, yes I am definite about it, okay, then it will slam the building, but watched your behind your back, I am but the zombies are not too far, from no they are about 100 feet and they grab my hand, don't let them catch I won't, and about a second now, then I been being pull into alls the direction and I was screaming for help and now I know that I were not be save and then the fireworks went off and they got distract and I ran so fast that I thought I were faint at that moment I knew that I had to be strong, or I would be dead meat, and I refuse to be that's ever and Joan and Stacy started to fire and they were falling to the ground, now I knew that I could count on my friends and I were be left behind and die in the street of zombies., and I ran up and I kissed Joan and Stacy and wanted to give a hug but the zombies were coming our ways and we ran and ran that day and so far we are surviving the Apocalypse, and we are the only one left and we are heading to find the ferry boat to take us to the main land and then we can go toe New Orleans and I heard that no one there came infection and no zombies around, and Stacy and Joan hold on to Peter and didn't let him go and we are not, do you hears me and mores things were falling from the sky and it was not a satellite but it was like comet or a falling stars but it was really lights and it just came and then we saw the zombies coming and we once again ran but we somehow got stuck in the smack of zombies and no way out and at that moment I was terrify to death and I knew that I had to beat them and I didn't wanted to die that day and I just ran and they follow me inside and I called out and Joan and Stacy got me out and I was save so far and I knew that I could go on my own. The street lights were out and you were the groaning sound of zombies and they were smelling us and then I told them about a shop that there were bow and arrows and that the gun make too much noise and they listens to me to the point and then we walks and looked around if it was clear and then I said to Peter that there is a white van and we can hideout in there until the zombies passing us by and Joan said that is a good ideas before we reach the dock and we will be ready to leave and will not have deal with zombies no more, about one hour later we escape the zombies and headed to the docks and we notice torn bodies everywhere and then a lion came out and it was a zombies lion and attack and almost got me but Peter got a stick and a bow and arrow and shot in the head and but then somehow it just came back to live and attack me and I said save yourself, and they said no you are coming on the boat ride with us, and then a second lion came from nowhere and got me again and but now it was too late and they could save me, and I told them to shoot me before I turned and they said sorry Joan, we didn't wants you do die today, but promise that you will tell my family what happened and Stacy said yes we will and then Joan die and about two hours later the boat came and we boarded and we just looked back and we didn't sees that place again and it seems like we were going to be fine but then suddenly we had to jump the boat because we were surrounded by the zombies and we swam to the shore and so far we were safe and then we walks through the woods and we find a cabin and we when inside and sat there and Peter got some fireworks and we were warm and later that night we saw them through the window and there were thousand out there and what are we going to do? Don't make sound, I won't! banged the doors and it got louder and louder and then it stop and then the door creak and then 10 zombies got inside and then tried to grab me and somehow snuck out and I was save I thought and then Peter barley got out alive.

Apocalypse Zombies

Well yes he barley make out life and this happened when we to get out the stores for supplies and there were threes of us and thought that moment was a good idea but it was wrong both of my friends got slaughter by the zombies and I was left alone to defend myself and at that times I thought I were been gone too but once again they I were end dead but I got lucky, but now I with Peter and we are the two survive and I don't know if we are going to make it and everywhere we went, we ran into zombies and but now we need to search for a new shelter this one got invaded by zombies and now we need a other place that we just have not too be find out by zombies and I feel that they smell us and that how they find us and I told Peter that we need to spread something that zombies wouldn't smell us and then we will be safe and the suggest was that we pick up a zombies and get that dead smell into ours clothes and make sure that it were not rain, but at this point I was not sure it were work or not but I am willing to survive, I am trying to says that we were trying not to become zombies dead meat and we just kept on going and then we reach the river and we when west and then north toward the highway and I told Peter that we might run into zombies in a city and he said that is non sense and he didn't listen to my advice and so we just continue going until we got into strict area that we were fired at and almost hit and at this moment I just hid in behind the bushes and so did Peter, but then we when then I saws that car parked and I shown Peter and he told me to run and I did and he follow me and I got inside but I didn't looked and I almost got grab by a zombie. About a minute the air raid and the sirens when off and I said go Peter and I am in back of you and don't worry I won't get caught and Peter looked around and push the zombie into the water but it came out fighting and I thought wow they are powerful zombies and but I couldn't really fight that one off and about a second later, Stacy jump in and somehow she found the sword and chop the zombies head off and but it still was moving and I knew that I had to put the sword into the brains, and now I saw more coming toward us and now I had to run and save my ass and meanwhile Peter was fighting and not losing the battle and then at that moment I threw the grenade and it blow up and they were flying everywhere and we were not safe yet.

But time was on ours side and I knew that not giving up and we were have a chance to lives but we loss our friends and we need to find other peoples, to go on, but also had to be careful, not too make loud sound and that probably were hears us, so Peter and I ran into zombies were adult and children and even dogs, and the dogs were the vicious kind that they were eat you up and spite you out and but I didn't relax until we got someplace safer and you know there is no place that likes when you trying to escape the zombies, and seem bleak, but I never gave up and we so far make it out but the apocalypse continue and but there is no end but there are only zombies and no place to hide or run in this case they are fence in and they are on the run and they seem stronger and I hope that they are not but it didn't end with us fighting the zombies and we had to deal with some advance zombies that were much smarter and did know how to fight and they just knew how to catch a live person, so they were called predator and they were the hungry bunch and we needed to run and run and hide, but there were too many of them and we were in the middle and I thought how to gets around it, but I thought it were not works but we need to act like zombies without feeling and escape. But Peter said that were never work and I said we need to tried it but Peter when along with it and then we were fine and we got away, but I was wrong, and somehow we got inside a shoe place and I thought we were stupid and Peter was right because we ended up with more zombies inside and I didn't like that at alls and that was a bad plan and Peter was mad at me.

Air Raid and sirens

When we got inside and there were zombies and then we heard the air raid and then there was a explosion and now I know that it was not good for us to be inside and around this area, and we heard helicopter and jets flying above our heads and they were shooting missiles and bomb and that almost hit us and I said we cannot stay here not for a moment, I know but if we go outside we will get hit and die. The building were burning and they the building collapse and at that moment I thought were be crush and but somehow we make it and it stop and we climb out and the zombies were dead and the air with the smoke make me choke and then at that point I didn't give up and just saw torn bodies about ten miles block and so I told Peter we better go and I didn't wants to get no radioactive, and die and he agree and I put a cover my face and so did Peter and once again the bomb came and we didn't hide and then but we didn't get hurt but we were out of the smoke and but Peter was coughing and blood was coming out of his mouth and he was infection and he said shoot me, but why I will get you help but it is too late for me, no it is not and Stacy was like dragging her feet and at that moment, Peter fell to the ground and the tanks came and they pointed guns at us and then I said I am fine but seems like my got hurt and then they said well miss your friend has the virus so we need to elimination him now,, we need to be under control and can you take him to the hospital and it is too late for him. Don't says that he is fine, no he is not and we need to get rid of him and miss do you have any bite, no I don't and I am fine so we need to check you out and they did and then they took Stacy to camp and shot Peter and threw him into the fire and burned with the rest of the zombies and meanwhile Stacy cried and said he was not sick and he just need medical help and you killed him, well he could have turned and killed us alls so we had no choice so we killed him and the virus were not spread.

I don't understand but he was fine and but after the air raid and somehow he got injure and fell and probably a zombie bit him and he didn't feel it and he were have turned and that is my explained and if you don't understand what going out in the world and you survive the zombies attack,. You are one lucky lady, thanks and I didn't sacrifice my friends and I didn't like losing my friends and then I just kept on fighting and then the special report came and I was ready and I just kept going I do understand but your not alone now and we will protection you and then she saw thousand of zombies behind the electric fence and now I was getting a bit nerve and I didn't want them to break it down and get me and then I went to bed and I kept one eye open and gun under the cover. Went I heard a sound and I just tried not too panic and but I did and I didn't trust the soldiers to protection me, I was alone and I knew how to handle myself and so I didn't need someone with muscle and machine gun to protection me so I just slept and I didn't sleep deep but really light and I just wanted to be ready if I had too and then I heard the sirens and one of the soldiers said the zombies are lose and locked your door and don't let anyone in and I said no I won't but would you give me a gun and he said you don't need one and somehow I just took out of his pocket and hid it and said I will be fine now, and he left and I just hid under the pillow and I just sat and watched and I heard screams and I also heard, wants brains and brains and at that moment, the door, someone was trying to unlock and I knew it must been a zombie at this point I jump out of the window and ran to the jeep and I was surrounded by zombies and zombies soldiers and now I just started up and put my foot on the petal and speed away and didn't looked back and drove for hours and hours and when I was safe I stop and caught my breathe. And then I continue driving away from Zombies zone and I was thirsty and hungry but I knew that I had to reach California and I were be safe.

Six month later

I still kept on driving and so far I was like all alone and no one to talked
to but I still kept going and I stop in the middle of the road and slept
there. one night, I thought I saw that light coming down and I knew
I was heading the wrong direction and I said to myself to head back east
and I was not thinking clear and I was confuse and I was not sure but then
I took a nap and then I woke up and I thought that everything was fine
but the epidemic was not over and but got worst and I was not in danger
at that moment but I was not going to take any chance at alls and just
continue my journey to unknown territory and I was risking my life and
at that point I didn't care. But the I saw the city and I knew that I had
stop and sees if I was on my ways then a big truck and it almost ran into
me and knew that I couldn't let him go through and I saw the military
standing guard and with machine and gun, and seems like they were going
to shoot and I saw barbwire and at that point and I couldn't turn around
and when toward the city and I had to shown my id and they let me in and
then I saw so many zombies and but I just kept going and the military said
you have a crew in this city and you cannot walks at night and if you do
you will gets shot, and we are under martial law, and then Stacy thought
why did I go in here and I was better off elsewhere and now I am trapped
inside this compound and I did the wrong decision about this place and I
am trying to sneak out but how I will have to distract them somehow and
why did I do this?

Everyone listens you are not allow to leaves this city without permission
and so if you leave you will gets shot, oh no, I need to escape if I claw under
the fence and I am small enough and I will squeeze in and then I will wear

dark clothes and hide and make sure the light won't sees me and then I will run for my life into the woods and make sure that I don't get shot.

Will the plan the work? I don't know but I am willing to tried.

Now it night and I am in one of the room and now I will change and then I will gets my stuff and my id and I will crawl under the fence and be freed once again, that were be great, one of the person heard me will tell the soldier and I need to find out who she is and keep her mouth shut and then I will tied her up and then I will escape and then Tina said take me with you and Stacy said no, I am not going anywhere, you are liar, no I am not.

Around midnight, Stacy got up and got dress and wash her face and got her stuff and also when into officer room to steal her id and then got her bag and snuck out the back door and then Tina follow her and was very quiet and then Stacy climb through the fence and over two fence to get across and when Tina tried and she fell and slip on her face and the dogs were barking and Tina got caught and they said where would planning to go? Just to sees the outside world, well we need to teach you lesson, I didn't do anything wrong, yes you did, you tried to runway and Tina didn't squeal on Stacy and pretend she was in her room. The next morning they search for her but she was no place insight. Stacy was walking in the desert for miles and miles and no sight but one dead bodies and seeing zombies with bloody mouth and hands and I need not too be seen and I knew that I was near my destiny and I know that I will find others peoples beside me and I was I losing ground and I thought let me make it and I don't wants to dies in the desert with snakes and raven flying over my head and I was starving and I was getting weaker and I thought I wouldn't make it to LA at this point I was someplace in Arizona , and I knew that I needed to find a car and drive the rest of the ways but my luck was not the best, and my friends are gone because of the virus and by the zombies and I know that if I got to LA and I would get some help and maybe a place to stay and hope that the epidemic didn't spread to LA, that I was hoping and but everything was silent, and I only thing that I saw was fire and burning and zombies coming toward me.

Now I ran into the desert and I thought I am in a open space and I will be spotted and I knew that I needed to hide out and it is not safe to be seen by anyone and so then I somehow I hid in the desert but it was a bit difficult and a few zombies were chasing me and ran and ran and I was out of breath and I knew that I was with zombies and not with the living and but with the night of the living of dead, and so I saw a cave and I couldn't believe it and then and I just when inside and then I just hide out for two days and the next day I continue the journey when on my own and I killed a snake and I ate a raw snake and because I was rally starving and but then I rested and the next day I left and continue and I when deeper and deeper and then I climb the hill and when around the mountain but I didn't sees a soul not at all and I kept out going and going and I got to some shack and I went inside and it had cobweb and spiders and other insects inside and the table with blood stains and I thought I am not staying long, but I rested and then I got up and continue walking and I didn't find no water and no foods and then I just couldn't make it and then I just sat for awhile and then I feel asleep in the middle of desert, the next minute I felt that I was not alone and then I got up and those were zombies , around me. I suddenly got up and at that moment I thought I was going to gets venous and I just ran of my life and then I kept going and then next I spotted the blue car and in the driveway and I looked around and I got inside and then I saw a dead body in the back seat and I remove it and it was not a zombie and so I just put on the ground and drove away and then I headed to the highway and I was headed to unknown origin and I didn't care at this point but I was going crazy talking too myself and I put on the radio, only emergency alert was on at this point I knew it was not over and I just had to drive and the tank was half full and I need to get some more gas to continue to LA.

I drove for about 100 miles and I then I rested and I continue journey.

Unknown origin

Now I stop for gas and then I filled up for gas and then I when toward to LA and I drove and I didn't stops for foods and then there was a "special bullets and they said stay off the highway zombies are on sight and be careful and caution and I now I was not sure at this point I was headed but I know that I had to get off the main road. On my ways I just saw places burning and a lot of explosion around me and a few times I thought that it was going to hit and it was really close and terrify time of my life and I need to defend on my own and I knew that I were not being rescue because I seem like I was alone at this point and but I didn't think about being negative but I just kept going and hoping and praying and talking to someone and I thought to myself I don't want to live in the world of zombies, now I make it but longer I don't know but I didn't wants to have any negative otherwise I would end up dead and I didn't want that neither and I just kept on driving and the highways were flooded with cars and I had to go around then and I also saw bodies lying there and I just couldn't looked at that point and I just kept driving and when I reach end of the highway and switch highway I saw a dozen of zombies. but I was not clear and I thought what were happen if I just stop and but that were be really crazy and taking a dangerous risk and I was not going to do that's and I just drove away and I didn't looked back and then some zombies tried to jump my car and I just kept on going and I pray that they were not gets on and I just gave a sharp turn and I kept on going and then I notice that they were on my tail and I needed to lose them in a hurried and I just drove like a crazy lady and I knew that I were not be caught by the police and I just didn't wanted to be in the middle of zombies and I just kept going to the bridge and I cross to Las Vega and I didn't sees any zombies at that point but I just kept going toward the casinos and then I park the car in the garage and I when in and I check around and I saw the kitchen and I when inside and I saw some foods in the fridge and I took some and it tasty good and I filled up my bag and then I heard . wants brains and I knew that I had to escape that moment and I ran into the corridor and I knew that I had to go to the elevator and gets out of that place immediately and I was like froze for a second and then I ran for my life and got going and then I ran into zombies dogs and cats and lions and tigers and now I was really scare and I didn't have a weapons to killed them but I kind of been quiet and snuck into my car and started up and they were coming closer too me and now I was frighten and but I still drove away and I just kept going and the lion jump on my car and I just somehow I got him off and I was relief and then cats and dogs and the zombies were chasing me and I need to opens the door from the garage and get the hell out and now the door were not open and I was not sure but it seems like it was short circuit and I didn't like being stuck with the zombies. but I just drove and then I saw the opening and I got out and I was not hungry at that time and I was ready to get too LA and then I would be safe and I thought but I could be wrong and I am will not think that ways until I sees if I did the right choice and then I will not be alone.

Alls the ways I was driving and I saw them and I just kept to be cool and then I was not going to fight without weapons I would lose.

Now it was about one hour later and I was headed on route 80 and I was relax and didn't panic and no more stops and then I had to stop and then I slept for awhile and then I woke up it was pouring rain and then got a little foggy and I just but on the light in the car and I continue driving to LA.

But I make a few stops and then I kept going and no one was on the road and but I was the only one on the highway and I just drove and drove until I got to some rest stop and wash my face and then I looked around and I was alone and no one to sees, and it was know one around.

Moon Eclipse, Day of Darkness

Soul Survive

One survive

Stacy drove for days and I did reach the LA border and I was about to enter and now I did and I don't know what my destiny will be but I just kept driving and they did warns that city were the most dangerous with zombies and I drove into Hollywood Boulevard and so far no sight of zombies and then I when near the Beverly center but the streets but I was seeing bodies parts and then the next street I saw zombies about thousand of them and now I was headed the farmer market and I couldn't believe there were zombies everywhere and then I heard groaning and moaning we wants brains, and now I knew that I had to head out of dodge and then I could be safe but I was all alone and I didn't have no place to go but to the Beverly center and hide out in one of the store and then I maybe find something to fight with but so far I didn't have no hope. But at that point I didn't give up and I know that I had to find a TV to listen to the later report about this epidemic and I was my choice so I went to electronic and I put on the TV but the power was off. But I find a generator and I plug in and the lights when on but then I thought I don't put a attention on me and I just turned it off and then I kept quiet but now I knew they got inside and I am not alone and then zombies and got to the high level and now I was afraid that I would get caught but I was not give up and I knew that I had to leave this place and but I stayed and I just thought and then I realize it was time to go to the San Diego and but were be better I don't know but I knew this place were be very danger to stay at night and would be able to escape so I just stood there and looked around and thought of plan now how to get out of here without being seen, but what were be my distract, yes I thought yes the lights and the elevator music that were keep the zombies going and they were much stronger and more advance then the East coast zombie and I could manage on my own to fight with them, just runs.

So that moment I did and ran for my life and I didn't looked back and got to the car and got out of Beverly center and headed to San Diego and saw the ocean with zombies walking and I said good I didn't stops here but I had few on my tail and they were reaching my car and I tried to drive quicker and the car skid near the edge and now I knew that I would end up dead if I didn't go slower but if I went fast probably were end up in the ocean and my car into flames, and I refuse to end that ways even though I was the only alive and I don't know how long I will live but I am just going until I don't runs into no more zombies, and but each turned I took there were zombies, and now I was a bit terrify, somehow I ended in territory of zombies and stops, and at this point I don't know but I did, was I losing it probably I did, but then I put my foot on the pedal and sped away and didn't looked back and drove over zombies and hours and hours to get to my destination and I knew that I would find someone but I was hoping but then I got tired and stop in the middle of the highway and rested a bit and then headed and didn't stop until I got there! about one hour I drove into San Diego and I was home and alone and at this point I cried and cried and know one there but stains and blood and bodies parts and then I turned the corner and I saw the zombies, and how I headed toward the beach and I didn't stop and I when by the mall and then I saw the building and said now I am home and then I parked the car and walks inside that building and I got into the lobby and took the stairs and open the door and know one was there and I stepped inside and I close and shut it tight and I just sat on the couch and sat and looked out and then a moment later I saw a cat but it was not a zombie and it jump on the couch. I pet the cat and the cat said meow and I fed the cat and I was just looking out and then I looked into the closet and for the change and I knew that the epidemic was not over.

For now I was safe and I am staying here for awhile. And time when by and nothing didn't change and so I stayed there for now. But I sometime I just looked out and got supplies and but I need to be on my watched and then I will be the only one that make it and but why and I don't understand, and I do go out to get stuff and then I just when out and sees if the zombies were gone but they were still around, but each day I find a gun and I thought if the zombies broke in I were shoot myself and not gets bitten and so, but I took one day a time and I just each day I woke up the population grew and I knew I was out numbered and I were never make it alive, and I thought being with the cat in some sense I was not alone and I were make it today and tomorrow, but I believe that zombies knew that I was here.

But I knew that I couldn't tell them know but I was very quiet but the cat was giving the zombies some kind of attention and I needed to keeps the cat quiet. Once again I stepped out and I left the cat behind and I search for guns and bullets and but I didn't find the any gun shop in the area and I knew that I were need to go further into the city but I had a fear that the zombies were follow me, and I knew they were I was there foods supply.

I when to the radio station to broadcast alive but know one was didn't hears me I was alone but I said I am in the high rise in San Diego and I am on the tenth floor, if anyone hear me, comes, and get me, but the zombies grew in numbered and I said no I am staying inside from now and not going outside and I do have everything that I have, and that night I when to sleep and hope that morning were be a better day but my foods was running out and I had no choice but stayed inside for now. Then I heard some kind of active and I knew that they were inside and I knew that they were going to found me so I decided to take the cat on the 23 floors and I check into and but I did not sees any dead body and it was clear and one thing the epidemic, and was still going on!!!! But I was safe for now.

Moon Eclipse, Day of Darkness

No ways out, the epidemic spread!

JEAN MARIE RUSIN, lives with her mom and brother in New Britain, Connecticut and also graduation from Connecticut school of broadcasting and graduation on September 7, 2007, and belonged to Authors and Publishers association, and also I do my own talked radio on blogtalkradio. com and my website is www.jeanmarierusin.com and Jean Marie Rusin, is on Face book and Jean Marie Rusin Fan Club and Jean Marie Rusin Fan Club Michigan branch and Jean is also on Twitter and My space .com.